Countess Kate

Charlotte M. Yonge

Contents

COUNTESS KATE

BY

Charlotte M. Yonge

CHAPTER I.

There, I've done every bit I can do! I'm going to see what o'clock it is."

"I heard it strike eleven just now."

"Sylvia, you'll tip up! What a tremendous stretch!"

"Wha-ooh! Oh dear! We sha'n't get one moment before dinner! Oh, horrible! oh, horrible! most horrible!"

"Sylvia, you know I hate hearing Hamlet profaned."

"You can't hate it more than having no one to hear our lessons."

"That makes you do it. What on earth can Mary be about?"

"Some tiresome woman to speak to her, I suppose."

"I'm sure it can't be as much her business as it is to mind her poor little sisters. Oh dear! if Papa could only afford us a governess!"

"I am sure I should not like it at all; besides, it is wrong to wish to be richer than one is."

"I don't wish; I am only thinking how nice it would be, if some one would give us a famous quantity of money. Then Papa should have a pretty parsonage, like the one at Shagton; and we would make the church beautiful, and get another pony or two, to ride with Charlie."

"Yes, and have a garden with a hothouse like Mr. Brown's."

"Oh yes; and a governess to teach us to draw. But best of all--O Sylvia! wouldn't it be nice not to have to mind one's clothes always? Yes, you laugh; but it comes easier to you; and, oh dear! oh dear! it is so horrid to be always having to see one does not tear oneself."

"I don't think you do see," said Sylvia, laughing.

"My frocks always WILL get upon the thorns. It is very odd."

"Only do please, Katie dear, let me finish this sum; and then if Mary is not come, she can't scold if we are amusing ourselves."

"I know!" cried Kate. "I'll draw such a picture, and tell you all about it when your sum is over."

Thereon ensued silence in the little room, half parlour, half study, nearly filled with books and piano; and the furniture, though carefully protected with brown holland, looking the worse for wear, and as if danced over by a good many young folks.

The two little girls, who sat on the opposite sides of a little square table in the bay-window, were both between ten and eleven years old, but could not have been taken for twins, nor even for sisters, so unlike were their features and complexion; though their dress, very dark grey linsey, and brown holland aprons, was exactly the same, except that Sylvia's was enlivened by scarlet braid, Kate's darkened by black--and moreover, Kate's apron was soiled, and the frock bore traces of a great darn. In fact, new frocks for the pair were generally made necessary by Kate's tattered state, when Sylvia's garments were still available for little Lily, or for some school child.

Sylvia's brown hair was smooth as satin; Kate's net did not succeed in confining the loose rough waves of dark chestnut, on the road to blackness. Sylvia was the shorter, firmer, and stronger, with round white well-cushioned limbs; Kate was tall, skinny, and brown, though perfectly healthful. The face of the one was round and rosy, of the other thin and dark; and one pair of eyes were of honest grey, while the others were large and hazel, with blue whites. Kate's little hand was so slight, that Sylvia's strong fingers could almost crush it together, but it was far less effective in any sort of handiwork; and her slim neatly-made foot always was a reproach to her for making such boisterous steps, and wearing out her shoes so much faster than the quieter movements of her companion did--her sister, as the children would have said, for nothing but the difference of surname reminded Katharine Umfraville that she was not the sister of Sylvia Wardour.

Her father, a young clergyman, had died before she could remember anything, and her mother had not survived him three months. Little Kate had then become the charge of her mother's sister, Mrs. Wardour, and had grown up in the little parsonage belonging to the district church of St. James's, Oldburgh, amongst her cousins, calling Mr. and Mrs. Wardour Papa and Mamma, and feeling no difference between their love to their own five children and to her.

Mrs. Wardour had been dead for about four years, and the little girls were taught by the eldest sister, Mary, who had been at a boarding- school to fit her for educating them. Mr. Wardour too taught them a good deal himself, and had the more time for them since Charlie, the youngest boy, had gone every day to the grammar-school in the town.

Armyn, the eldest of the family, was with Mr. Brown, a very good old solicitor, who, besides his office in Oldburgh, had a very pretty house and grounds two miles beyond St. James's, where the parsonage children were delighted to spend an afternoon now and then.

Little did they know that it was the taking the little niece as a daughter that had made it needful to make Armyn enter on a profession at once, instead of going to the university and becoming a clergyman like his father; nor how cheerfully Armyn had agreed to do whatever would best lighten his father's cares and troubles. They were a very happy family; above all, on the Saturday evenings and Sundays that the good-natured elder brother spent at home.

"There!" cried Sylvia, laying down her slate pencil, and indulging in another tremendous yawn; "we can't do a thing more till Mary comes! What can she be about?"

"Oh, but look, Sylvia!" cried Kate, quite forgetting everything in the interest of her drawing on a large sheet of straw-paper. "Do you see what it is?"

"I don't know," said Sylvia, "unless--let me see--That's a very rich little girl, isn't it?" pointing to an outline of a young lady whose wealth was denoted by the flounces (or rather scallops) on her frock, the bracelets on her sausage-shaped arms, and the necklace on her neck.

"Yes; she is a very rich and grand--Lady Ethelinda; isn't that a pretty name? I do wish I was Lady Katharine."

"And what is she giving? I wish you would not do men and boys, Kate; their legs always look so funny as you do them."

"They never will come right; but never mind, I must have them. That is Lady Ethelinda's dear good cousin, Maximilian; he is a lawyer-- don't you see the parchment sticking out of his pocket?"

"Just like Armyn."

"And she is giving him a box with a beautiful new microscope in it; don't you see the top of it? And there is a whole pile of books. And I would draw a pony, only I never can nicely; but look here,"-- Kate went on drawing as she spoke--"here is Lady Ethelinda with her best hat on, and a little girl coming. There is the little girl's house, burnt down; don't you see?"

Sylvia saw with the eyes of her mind the ruins, though her real eyes saw nothing but two lines, meant to be upright, joined together by a wild zig-zag, and with some peaked scrabbles and round whirls intended for smoke. Then Kate's ready pencil portrayed the family, as jagged in their drapery as the flames and presently Lady Ethelinda appeared before a counter (such a counter! sloping like a desk in the attempt at perspective, but it conveniently concealed the shopman's legs,) buying very peculiar garments for the sufferers. Another scene in which she was presenting them followed, Sylvia looking on, and making suggestions; for in fact there was no quiet pastime more relished by the two cousins than drawing stories, as they called it, and most of their pence went in paper for that purpose.

"Lady Ethelinda had a whole ream of paper to draw on!" were the words pronounced in Kate's shrill key of eagerness, just as the long lost Mary and her father opened the door.

"Indeed!" said Mr. Wardour, a tall, grave-looking man; "and who is Lady Ethelinda!"

"O Papa, it's just a story I was drawing," said Kate, half eager, half ashamed.

"We have done all the lessons we could, indeed we have--" began Sylvia; "my music and our French grammar, and--"

"Yes, I know," said Mary; and she paused, looking embarrassed and uncomfortable, so that Sylvia stood in suspense and wonder.

"And so my little Kate likes thinking of Lady--Lady Etheldredas," said Mr. Wardour rather musingly; but Kate was too much pleased at his giving any sort of heed to her performances to note the manner, and needed no more encouragement to set her tongue off.

"Lady Ethelinda, Papa. She is a very grand rich lady, though she is a little girl: and see there, she is giving presents to all her cousins; and there she is buying new clothes for the orphans that were burnt out; and there she is building a school for them."

Kate suddenly stopped, for Mr. Wardour sat down, drew her between his knees, took both her hands into one of his, and looked earnestly into her face, so gravely that she grew frightened, and looking appealingly up, cried out, "O Mary, Mary! have I been naughty?"

"No, my dear," said Mr. Wardour; "but we have heard a very strange piece of news about you, and I am very anxious as to whether it may turn out for your happiness."

Kate stood still and looked at him, wishing he would speak faster. Could her great-uncle in India be come home, and want her to make him a visit in London? How delightful! If it had been anybody but Papa, she would have said, "Go on."

"My dear," said Mr. Wardour at last, "you know that your cousin, Lord Caergwent, was killed by an accident last week."

"Yes, I know," said Kate; "that was why Mary made me put this black braid on my frock; and a very horrid job it was to do--it made my fingers so sore."

"I did not know till this morning that his death would make any other difference to you," continued Mr. Wardour. "I thought the title went to heirs-male, and that Colonel Umfraville was the present earl; but, my little Katharine, I find that it is ordained that you should have this great responsibility."

"What, you thought it was the Salic law?" said Kate, going on with one part of his speech, and not quite attending to the other.

"Something like it; only that it is not the English term for it," said Mr. Wardour, half smiling. "As your grandfather was the elder son, the title and property come to you."

Kate did not look at him, but appeared intent on the marks of the needle on the end of her forefinger, holding down her head.

Sylvia, however, seemed to jump in her very skin, and opening her eyes, cried out, "The title! Then Kate is--is--oh, what is a she- earl called?"

"A countess," said Mr. Wardour, with a smile, but rather sadly. "Our little Kate is Countess of Caergwent."

"My dear Sylvia!" exclaimed Mary in amazement; for Sylvia, like an India-rubber ball, had bounded sheer over the little arm-chair by which she was standing.

But there her father's look and uplifted finger kept her still and silent. He wanted to give Kate time to understand what he had said.

"Countess of Caergwent," she repeated; "that's not so pretty as if I were Lady Katharine."

"The sound does not matter much," said Mary. "You will always be Katharine to those that love you best. And oh!--" Mary stopped short, her eyes full of tears.

Kate looked up at her, astonished. "Are you sorry, Mary?" she asked, a little hurt.

"We are all sorry to lose our little Kate," said Mr. Wardour.

"Lose me, Papa!" cried Kate, clinging to him, as the children scarcely ever did, for he seldom made many caresses; "Oh no, never! Doesn't Caergwent Castle belong to me? Then you must all come and live with me there; and you shall have lots of big books, Papa; and we will have a pony-carriage for Mary, and ponies for Sylvia and Charlie and me, and--"

Kate either ran herself down, or saw that the melancholy look on Mr. Wardour's face rather deepened than lessened, for she stopped short.

"My dear," he said, "you and I have both other duties."

"Oh," but if I built a church! I dare say there are people at Caergwent as poor as they are here. Couldn't we build a church, and you mind them, Papa?"

"My little Katharine, you have yet to understand that 'the heir, so long as he is a child, differeth in nothing from a servant, but is under tutors and governors.' You will not have any power over yourself or your property till you are twenty-one."

"But you are my tutor and my governor, and my spiritual pastor and master," said Kate. "I always say so whenever Mary asks us questions about our duty to our neighbour."

"I have been so hitherto," said Mr. Wardour, setting her on his knee; "but I see I must explain a good deal to you. It is the business of a court in London, that is called the Court of Chancery, to provide that proper care is taken of young heirs and heiresses and their estates, if no one have been appointed by their parents to do so; and it is this court that must settle what is to become of you."

"And why won't it settle that I may live with my own papa and brothers and sisters?"

"Because, Kate, you must be brought up in a way to fit your station; and my children must be brought up in a way to fit theirs. And besides," he added more sadly, "nobody that could help it would leave a girl to be brought up in a household without a mother."

Kate's heart said directly, that as she could never again have a mother, her dear Mary must be better than a stranger; but somehow any reference to the sorrow of the household always made her anxious to get away from the subject, so she looked at her finger again, and asked, "Then am I to live up in this Court of Chances?"

"Not exactly," said Mr. Wardour. "Your two aunts in London, Lady Barbara and Lady Jane Umfraville, are kind enough to offer to take charge of you. Here is a letter that they sent inclosed for you."

"The Countess of Caergwent," was written on the envelope; and Kate's and Sylvia's heads were together in a moment to see how it looked, before opening the letter, and reading:- "'My dear Niece,'--dear me, how funny to say niece!--'I deferred writing to you upon the melancholy--' oh, what is it, Sylvia?"

"The melancholy comet!"

"No, no; nonsense."

"Melancholy event," suggested Mary.

"Yes, to be sure. I can't think why grown-up people always write on purpose for one not to read them.--'Melancholy event that has placed you in possession of the horrors of the family.'"

"Horrors!--Kate, Kate!"

"Well, I am sure it IS horrors," said the little girl rather perversely.

"This is not a time for nonsense, Kate," said Mr. Wardour; and she was subdued directly.

"Shall I read it to you?" said Mary.

"Oh, no, no!" Kate was too proud of her letter to give it up, and applied herself to it again.--'"Family honours, until I could ascertain your present address. And likewise, the shock of your poor cousin's death so seriously affected my sister's health in her delicate state, that for some days I could give my attention to nothing else.' Dear me! This is my Aunt Barbara, I see! Is Aunt Jane so ill?"

"She has had very bad health for many years," said Mr. Wardour; "and your other aunt has taken the greatest care of her."

"'We have now, however, been able to consider what will be best for all parties; and we think nothing will be so proper as that you should reside with us for the present. We will endeavour to make a happy home for you; and will engage a lady to superintend your education, and give you all the advantages to which you are entitled. We have already had an interview with a very admirable person, who will come down to Oldburgh with our butler next Friday, and escort you to us, if Mrs. Wardour will kindly prepare you for the journey. I have written to thank her for her kindness to you.'"

"Mrs. Wardour!" exclaimed Sylvia.

"The ladies have known and cared little about Kate or us for a good many years," said Mary, almost to herself, but in such a hurt tone, that her father looked up with grave reproof in his eyes, as if to remind her of all he had been saying to her during the long hours that the little girls had waited.

"'With your Aunt Jane's love, and hoping shortly to be better acquainted, I remain, my dear little niece, your affectionate aunt, Barbara Umfraville.' Then I am to go and live with them!" said Kate, drawing a long sigh. "O Papa, do let Sylvia come too, and learn of my governess with me!"

"Your aunts do not exactly contemplate that," said Mr. Wardour; "but perhaps there may be visits between you."

Sylvia began to look very grave. She had not understood that this great news was to lead to nothing but separation. Everything had hitherto been in common between her and Kate, and that what was good for the one should not be good for the other was so new and strange, that she did not understand it at once.

"Oh yes! we will visit. You shall all come and see me in London, and see the Zoological Gardens and the British Museum; and I will send you such presents!"

"We will see," said Mr. Wardour kindly; "but just now, I think the best thing you can do is to write to your aunt, and thank her for her kind letter; and say that I will bring you up to London on the day she names, without troubling the governess and the butler."

"Oh, thank you!" said Kate; "I sha'n't be near so much afraid if you come with me."

Mr. Wardour left the room; and the first thing Mary did was to throw her arms round the little girl in a long vehement embrace. "My little Kate! my little Kate! I little thought this was to be the end of it!" she cried, kissing her, while the tears dropped fast.

Kate did not like it at all. The sight of strong feeling distressed her, and made her awkward and ungracious. "Don't, Mary," she said, disengaging herself; "never mind; I shall always come and see you; and when I grow up, you shall come to live with me at Caergwent. And you know, when they write a big red book about me, they will put in that you brought me up."

"Write a big red book about you, Kate!"

"Why," said Kate, suddenly become very learned, "there is an immense fat red and gold book at Mr. Brown's, all full of Lords and Ladies."

"Oh, a Peerage!" said Mary; "but even you, my Lady Countess, can't have a whole peerage to yourself."

And that little laugh seemed to do Mary good, for she rose and began to rule the single lines for Kate's letter. Kate could write a very tidy little note; but just now she was too much elated and excited to sit down quietly, or quite to know what she was about. She went skipping restlessly about from one chair to another, chattering fast about what she would do, and wondering what the aunts would be like, and what Armyn would say, and what Charlie would say, and the watch she would buy for Charlie, and the great things she was to do for everybody--till Mary muttered something in haste, and ran out of the room.

"I wonder why Mary is so cross," said Kate.

Poor Mary! No one could be farther from being cross; but she was thoroughly upset. She was as fond of Kate as of her own sisters, and was not only sorry to part with her, but was afraid that she would not be happy or good in the new life before her.

CHAPTER II.

The days passed very slowly with Kate, until the moment when she was to go to London and take her state upon her, as she thought. Till that should come to pass, she could not feel herself really a countess. She did not find herself any taller or grander; Charlie teased her rather more instead of less and she did not think either Mr. Wardour or Mary or Armyn thought half enough of her dignity: they did not scruple to set her down when she talked too loud, and looked sad instead of pleased when she chattered about the fine things she should do. Mr. and Mrs. Brown, to be sure, came to wish her good-bye; but they were so respectful, and took such pains that she should walk first, that she grew shy and sheepish, and did not like it at all.

She thought ease and dignity would come by nature when she was once in London; and she made so certain of soon seeing Sylvia again, that she did not much concern herself about the parting with her; while she was rather displeased with Mary for looking grave, and not making more of her, and trying to tell her that all might not be as delightful as she expected. She little knew that Mary was grieved at her eagerness to leave her happy home, and never guessed at the kind sister's fears for her happiness. She set it all down to what she was wont to call crossness. If Mary had really been a cross or selfish person, all she would have thought of would have been that now there would not be so many rents to mend after Kate's cobbling attempts, nor so many shrill shrieking laughs to disturb Papa writing his sermon, nor so much difficulty in keeping any room in the house tidy, nor so much pinching in the housekeeping. Instead of that, Mary only thought whether Barbara and Lady Jane would make her little Kate happy and good. She was sure they were proud, hard, cold people; and her father had many talks with her, to try to comfort her about them.

Mr. Wardour told her that Kate's grandfather had been such a grief and shame to the family, that it was no wonder they had not liked to be friendly with those he had left behind him. There had been help given to educate the son, and some notice had been taken of him, but always very distant; and he had been thought very foolish for marrying when he was very young, and very ill off. At the time of his death, his uncle, Colonel Umfraville, had been very kind, and had consulted earnestly with Mr. Wardour what was best for the little orphan; but had then explained that he and his wife could not take charge of her, because his regiment was going to India, and she could not go there with them; and that his sisters were prevented from undertaking the care of so young a child by the bad health of the elder, who almost owed her life to the tender nursing of the younger. And as Mrs. Wardour was only eager to keep to herself all that was left of her only sister, and had a nursery of her own, it had been most natural that Kate should remain at St. James's Parsonage; and Mr. Wardour had full reason to believe that, had there been any need, or if he had asked for help, the aunts would have gladly given it. He knew them to be worthy and religious women; and he told Mary that he thought it very likely that they might deal better with Kate's character than he had been able to do. Mary knew she herself had made mistakes, but she could not be humble for her father, or think any place more improving than under his roof.

And Kate meanwhile had her own views. And when all the good-byes were over, and she sat by the window of the railway carriage, watching the fields rush by, reduced to silence, because "Papa" had told her he could not hear her voice, and had made a peremptory sign to her when she screamed her loudest, and caused their fellow- travellers to look up amazed, she wove a web in her brain something like this:- "I know what my aunts will be like: they will be just like ladies in a book. They will be dreadfully fashionable! Let me see--Aunt Barbara will have a turban on her head, and a bird of paradise, like the bad old lady in Armyn's book that Mary took away from me; and they will do nothing all day long but try on flounced gowns, and count their jewels, and go out to balls and operas--and they will want me to do the same--and play at cards all Sunday! 'Lady Caergwent,' they will say, 'it is becoming to your position!' And then the young countess presented a remarkable contrast in her ingenuous simplicity," continued Kate, not quite knowing whether she was making a story or thinking of herself--for indeed she did not feel as if she were herself, but somebody in a story. "Her waving hair was only confined by an azure ribbon, (Kate loved a fine word when Charlie did not hear it to laugh at her;) and her dress was of the simplest muslin, with one diamond aigrette of priceless value!"

Kate had not the most remote notion what an aigrette might be, but she thought it would sound well for a countess; and she went on musing very pleasantly on the amiable simplicity of the countess, and the speech that was to cure the aunts of playing at cards on a Sunday, wearing turbans, and all other enormities, and lead them to live in the country, giving a continual course of school feasts, and surprising meritorious families with gifts of cows. She only wished she had a pencil to draw it all to show Sylvia, provided Sylvia would know her cows from her tables.

After more vain attempts at chatter, and various stops at stations, Mr. Wardour bought a story-book for her; and thus brought her to a most happy state of silent content, which lasted till the house roofs of London began to rise on either side of the railway.

Among the carriages that were waiting at the terminus was a small brougham, very neat and shiny; and a servant came up and touched his hat, opening the door for Kate, who was told to sit there while the servant and Mr. Wardour looked for the luggage. She was a little disappointed. She had once seen a carriage go by with four horses, and a single one did not seem at all worthy of her; but she had two chapters more of her story to read, and was so eager to see the end of it, that Mr. Wardour could hardly persuade her to look out and see the Thames when she passed over it, nor the Houses of Parliament and the towers of Westminster Abbey.

At last, while passing through the brighter and more crowded streets, Kate having satisfied herself what had become of the personages of her story, looked up, and saw nothing but dull houses of blackened cream colour; and presently found the carriage stopping at the door of one.

"Is it here, Papa?" she said, suddenly seized with fright.

"Yes," he said, "this is Bruton Street;" and he looked at her anxiously as the door was opened and the steps were let down. She took tight hold of his hand. Whatever she had been in her day- dreams, she was only his own little frightened Kate now; and she tried to shrink behind him as the footman preceded them up the stairs, and opening the door, announced--"Lady Caergwent and Mr. Wardour!"

Two ladies rose up, and came forward to meet her. She felt herself kissed by both, and heard greetings, but did not know what to say, and stood up by Mr. Wardour, hanging down her head, and trying to stand upon one foot with the other, as she always did when she was shy and awkward.

"Sit down, my dear," said one of the ladies, making a place for her on the sofa. But Kate only laid hold of a chair, pulled it as close to Mr. Wardour as possible, and sat down on the extreme corner of it, feeling for a rail on which to set her feet, and failing to find one, twining her ankles round the leg of the chair. She knew very well that this was not pretty; but she never could recollect what was pretty behaviour when she was shy. She was a very different little girl in a day-dream and out of one. And when one of the aunts asked her if she were tired, all she could do was to give a foolish sort of smile, and say, "N--no."

Then she had a perception that Papa was looking reprovingly at her; so she wriggled her legs away from that of the chair, twisted them together in the middle, and said something meant for "No, thank you;" but of which nothing was to be heard but "q," apparently proceeding out of the brim of her broad hat, so low did the young countess, in her amiable simplicity, hold her head.

"She is shy!" said one of the ladies to the other; and they let her alone a little, and began to talk to Mr. Wardour about the journey, and various other things, to which Kate did not greatly listen. She began to let her eyes come out from under her hat brim, and satisfied herself that the aunts certainly did not wear either turbans or birds of paradise, but looked quite as like other people as she felt herself, in spite of her title.

Indeed, one aunt had nothing on her head at all but a little black velvet and lace, not much more than Mary sometimes wore, and the other only a very light cap. Kate thought great-aunts must be as old at least as Mrs. Brown, and was much astonished to see that these ladies had no air of age about them. The one who sat on the sofa had a plump, smooth, pretty, pink and white face, very soft and pleasant to look at, though an older person than Kate would have perceived that the youthful delicacy of the complexion showed that she had been carefully shut up and sheltered from all exposure and exertion, and that the quiet innocent look of the small features was that of a person who had never had to use her goodness more actively than a little baby. Kate was sure that this was aunt Jane, and that she should get on well with her, though that slow way of speaking was rather wearisome.

The other aunt, who was talking the most, was quite as slim as Mary, and had a bright dark complexion, so that if Kate had not seen some shades of grey in her black hair, it would have been hard to believe her old at all. She had a face that put Kate in mind of a picture of a beautiful lady in a book at home--the eyes, forehead, nose, and shape of the chin, were so finely made; and yet there was something in them that made the little girl afraid, and feel as if the plaster cast of Diana's head on the study mantelpiece had got a pair of dark eyes, and was looking very hard at her; and there was a sort of dry sound in her voice that was uncomfortable to hear.

Then Kate took a survey of the room, which was very prettily furnished, with quantities of beautiful work of all kinds, and little tables and brackets covered with little devices in china and curiosities under glass, and had flowers standing in the windows; and by the time she had finished trying to make out the subject of a print on the walls, she heard some words that made her think that her aunts were talking of her new governess, and she opened her ears to hear, "So we thought it would be an excellent arrangement for her, poor thing!" and "Papa" answering, "I hope Kate may try to be a kind considerate pupil." Then seeing by Kate's eyes that her attention had been astray, or that she had not understood Lady Barbara's words, he turned to her, saying, "Did you not hear what your aunt was telling me?"

"No, Papa."

"She was telling me about the lady who will teach you. She has had great afflictions. She has lost her husband, and is obliged to go out as governess, that she may be able to send her sons to school. So, Kate, you must think of this, and try to give her as little trouble as possible."

It would have been much nicer if Kate would have looked up readily, and said something kind and friendly; but the fit of awkwardness had come over her again, and with it a thought so selfish, that it can hardly be called otherwise than naughty--namely, that grown-up people in trouble were very tiresome, and never let young ones have any fun.

"Shall I take you to see Mrs. Lacy, my dear?" said Lady Barbara, rising. And as Kate took hold of Mr. Wardour's hand, she added, "You will see Mr. Wardour again after dinner. You had better dress, and have some meat for your tea, with Mrs. Lacy, and then come into the drawing-room."

This was a stroke upon Kate. She who had dined with the rest of the world ever since she could remember--she, now that she was a countess, to be made to drink tea up-stairs like a baby, and lose all that time of Papa's company! She swelled with displeasure: but Aunt Barbara did not look like a person whose orders could be questioned, and "Papa" said not a word in her favour. Possibly the specimen of manners she had just given had not led either him or Lady Barbara to think her fit for a late dinner.

Lady Barbara first took her up-stairs, and showed her a little long narrow bed-room, with a pretty pink-curtained bed in it.

"This will be your room, my dear," she said. "I am sorry we have not a larger one to offer you; but it opens into mine, as you see, and my sister's is just beyond. Our maid will dress you for a few days, when I hope to engage one for you."

Here was something like promotion! Kate dearly loved to have herself taken off her own hands, and not to be reproved by Mary for untidiness, or roughly set to rights by Lily's nurse. She actually exclaimed, "Oh, thank you!" And her aunt waited till the hat and cloak had been taken off and the chestnut hair smoothed, looked at her attentively, and said, "Yes, you are like the family."

"I'm very like my own papa," said Kate, growing a little bolder, but still speaking with her head on one side, which was her way when she said anything senti-mental.

"I dare say you are," answered her aunt, with the dry sound. "Are you ready now? I will show you the way. The house is very small," continued Lady Barbara, as they went down the stairs to the ground floor; "and this must be your school-room for the present."

It was the room under the back drawing-room; and in it was a lady in a widow's cap, sitting at work. "Here is your little Pupil--Lady Caergwent--Mrs. Lacy," said Lady Barbara. "I hope you will find her a good child. She will drink tea with you, and then dress, and afterwards I hope, we shall see you with her in the drawing-room."

Mrs. Lacy bowed, without any answer in words, only she took Kate's hand and kissed her. Lady Barbara left them, and there was a little pause. Kate looked at her governess, and her heart sank, for it was the very saddest face she had ever seen--the eyes looked soft and gentle, but as if they had wept till they could weep no longer; and when the question was asked, "Are you tired, my dear?" it was in a sunk tone, trying to be cheerful but the sadder for that very reason. Poor lady! it was only that morning that she had parted with her son, and had gone away from the home where she had lived with her husband and children.

Kate was almost distressed; yet she felt more at her ease than with her aunts, and answered, "Not at all, thank you," in her natural tone.

"Was it a long journey?"

Kate had been silent so long, that her tongue was ready for exertion; and she began to chatter forth all the events of the journey, without heeding much whether she were listened to or not, till having come to the end of her breath, she saw that Mrs. Lacy was leaning back in her chair, her eyes fixed as if her attention had gone away. Kate thereupon roamed round the room, peeped from the window and saw that it looked into a dull black-looking narrow garden, and then studied the things in the room. There was a piano, at which she shook her head. Mary had tried to teach her music; but after a daily fret for six weeks, Mr. Wardour had said it was waste of time and temper for both; and Kate was delighted. Then she came to a book-case; and there the aunts had kindly placed the books of their own younger days, some of which she had never seen before. When she had once begun on the "Rival Crusoes," she gave Mrs. Lacy no more trouble, except to rouse her from it to drink her tea, and then go and be dressed.

The maid managed the white muslin so as to make her look very nice; but before she had gone half way down-stairs, there was a voice behind--"My Lady! my Lady!"

She did not turn, not remembering that she herself must be meant; and the maid, running after her, caught her rather sharply, and showed her her own hand, all black and grimed.

"How tiresome!" cried she. "Why, I only just washed it!"

"Yes, my Lady; but you took hold of the balusters all the way down. And your forehead! Bless me! what would Lady Barbara say?"

For Kate had been trying to peep through the balusters into the hall below, and had of course painted her brow with London blacks. She made one of her little impatient gestures, and thought she was very hardly used--dirt stuck upon her, and brambles tore her like no one else.

She got safely down this time, and went into the drawing-room with Mrs.

Lacy, there taking a voyage of discovery among the pretty things, knowing she must not touch, but asking endless questions, some of which Mrs. Lacy answered in her sad indifferent way, others she could not answer, and Kate was rather vexed at her not seeming to care to know. Kate had not yet any notion of caring for other people's spirits and feelings; she never knew what to do for them, and so tried to forget all about them.

The aunts came in, and with them Mr. Wardour. She was glad to run up to him, and drag him to look at a group in white Parian under a glass, that had delighted her very much. She knew it was Jupiter's Eagle; but who was feeding it? "Ganymede," said Mr. Wardour; and Kate, who always liked mythological stories, went on most eagerly talking about the legend of the youth who was borne away to be the cup-bearer of the gods. It was a thing to make her forget about the aunts and everybody else; and Mr. Wardour helped her out, as he generally did when her talk was neither foolish nor ill-timed but he checked her when he thought she was running on too long, and went himself to talk to Mrs. Lacy, while Kate was obliged to come to her aunts, and stood nearest to Lady Jane, of whom she was least afraid.

"You seem quite at home with all the heathen gods, my dear," said Lady Jane; "how come you to know them so well?"

"In Charlie's lesson-books, you know," said Kate; and seeing that her aunt did not know, she went on to say, "there are notes and explanations. And there is a Homer--an English one, you know; and we play at it."

"We seem to have quite a learned lady here!" said aunt Barbara, in the voice Kate did not like. "Do you learn music?"

"No; I haven't got any ear; and I hate it!"

"Oh!" said Lady Barbara drily; and Kate seeing Mr. Wardour's eyes fixed on her rather anxiously, recollected that hate was not a proper word, and fell into confusion.

"And drawing?" said her aunt.

"No; but I want to--"

"Oh!" again said Lady Barbara, looking at Kate's fingers, which in her awkwardness she was apparently dislocating in a method peculiar to herself.

However, it was soon over, for it was already later than Kate's home bed-time; she bade everyone good-night, and was soon waited on by Mrs. Bartley, the maid, in her own luxurious little room.

But luxurious as it was, Kate for the first time thoroughly missed home. The boarded floor, the old crib, the deal table, would have been welcome, if only Sylvia had been there. She had never gone to bed without Sylvia in her life. And now she thought with a pang that Sylvia was longing for her, and looking at her empty crib, thinking too, it might be, that Kate had cared more for her grandeur than for the parting.

Not only was it sorrowful to be lonely, but also Kate was one of the silly little girls, to whom the first quarter of an hour in bed was a time of fright. Sylvia had no fears, and always accounted for the odd noises and strange sights that terrified her companion. She never believed that the house was on fire, even though the moon made very bright sparkles; she always said the sounds were the servants, the wind, or the mice; and never would allow that thieves would steal little girls, or anything belonging to themselves. Or if she were fast asleep, her very presence gave a feeling of protection.

But when the preparations were very nearly over, and Kate began to think of the strange room, and the roar of carriages in the streets sounded so unnatural, her heart failed her, and the fear of being alone quite overpowered her dread of the grave staid Mrs. Bartley, far more of being thought a silly little girl.

"Please please, Mrs. Bartley," she said in a trembling voice, "are you going away?"

"Yes, my Lady; I am going down to supper, when I have placed my Lady Jane's and my Lady Barbara's things."

"Then please--please," said Kate, in her most humble and insinuating voice, "do leave the door open while you are doing it."

"Very well, my Lady," was the answer, in a tone just like that in which Lady Barbara said "Oh!"

And the door stayed open; but Kate could not sleep. There seemed to be the rattle and bump of the train going on in her bed; the gas- lights in the streets below came in unnaturally, and the noises were much more frightful and unaccountable than any she had ever heard at home. Her eyes spread with fright, instead of clos-ing in sleep; then came the longing yearning for Sylvia, and tears grew hot in them; and by the time Mrs. Bartley had finished her preparations, and gone down, her distress had grown so unbearable, that she absolutely began sobbing aloud, and screaming, "Papa!" She knew he would be very angry, and that she should hear that such folly was shameful in a girl of her age; but any anger would be better than this dreadful loneliness. She screamed louder and louder; and she grew half frightened, half relieved, when she heard his step, and a buzz of voices on the stairs; and then there he was, standing by her, and saying gravely, "What is the matter, Kate?"

"O Papa, Papa, I want--I want Sylvia!--I am afraid!" Then she held her breath, and cowered under the clothes, ready for a scolding; but it was not his angry voice. "Poor child!" he said quietly and sadly. "You must put away this childishness, my dear. You know that you are not really alone, even in a strange place."

"No, no, Papa; but I am afraid--I cannot bear it!"

"Have you said the verse that helps you to bear it, Katie?"

"I could not say it without Sylvia."

She heard him sigh; and then he said, "You must try another night, my Katie, and think of Sylvia saying it at home in her own room. You will meet her prayers in that way. Now let me hear you say it."

Kate repeated, but half choked with sobs, "I lay me down in peace," and the rest of the calm words, with which she had been taught to lay herself in bed; but at the end she cried, "O Papa, don't go!"

"I must go, my dear: I cannot stay away from your aunts. But I will tell you what to do to-night, and other nights when I shall be away: say to yourself the ninety-first Psalm. I think you know it--'Whoso abideth under the defence of the Most High--'"

"I think I do know it."

"Try to say it to yourself, and then the place will seem less dreary, because you will feel Who is with you. I will look in once more before I go away, and I think you will be asleep."

And though Kate tried to stay awake for him, asleep she was.

CHAPTER III.

In a very few days, Kate had been settled into the ways of the household in Bruton Street; and found one day so like another, that she sometimes asked herself whether she had not been living there years instead of days.

She was always to be ready by half-past seven. Her French maid, Josephine, used to come in at seven, and wash and dress her quietly, for if there were any noise Aunt Barbara would knock and be displeased. Aunt Barbara rose long before that time, but she feared lest Aunt Jane should be disturbed in her morning's sleep; and Kate thought she had the ears of a dragon for the least sound of voice or laugh.

At half-past seven, Kate met Mrs. Lacy in the school-room, read the Psalms and Second Lesson, and learnt some answers to questions on the Catechism, to be repeated to Lady Barbara on a Sunday. For so far from playing at cards in a bird-of-paradise turban all Sunday, the aunts were quite as particular about these things as Mr. Wardour-- more inconveniently so, the countess thought; for he always let her answer his examinations out of her own head, and never gave her answers to learn by heart; "Answers that I know before quite well," said Kate, "only not made tiresome with fine words."

"That is not a right way of talking, Lady Caergwent," gravely said Mrs. Lacy; and Kate gave herself an ill-tempered wriggle, and felt cross and rebellious.

It was a trial; but if Kate had taken it humbly, she would have found that even the stiff hard words and set phrases gave accuracy to her ideas; and the learning of the texts quoted would have been clear gain, if she had been in a meeker spirit.

This done, Mrs. Lacy gave her a music-lesson. This was grievous work, for the question was not how the learning should be managed, but whether the thing should be learnt at all.

Kate had struggled hard against it. She informed her aunts that Mary had tried to teach her for six weeks in vain, and that she had had a bad mark every day; that Papa had said it was all nonsense, and that talents could not be forced; and that Armyn said she had no more ear than an old pea-hen.

To which Lady Barbara had gravely answered, that Mr. Wardour could decide as he pleased while Katharine was under his charge, but that it would be highly improper that she should not learn the accomplishments of her station.

"Only I can't learn," said Kate, half desperate; "you will see that it is no use, Aunt Barbara."

"I shall do my duty, Katharine," was all the answer she obtained; and she pinched her chair with suppressed passion.

Lady Barbara was right in saying that it was her duty to see that the child under her charge learnt what is usually expected of ladies; and though Kate could never acquire music enough to give pleasure to others, yet the training and discipline were likely not only to improve her ear and untamed voice, but to be good for her whole character--that is, if she had made a good use of them. But in these times, being usually already out of temper with the difficult answers of the Catechism questions, and obliged to keep in her pettish feelings towards what concerned sacred things, she let all out in the music lesson, and with her murmurs and her inattention, her yawns and her blunders, rendered herself infinitely more dull and unmusical than nature had made her, and was a grievous torment to poor Mrs. Lacy, and her patient, "One, two, three--now, my dear."

Kate thought it was Mrs. Lacy who tormented her! I wonder which was the worse to the other! At any rate, Mrs. Lacy's heavy eyes looked heavier, and she moved as though wearied out for the whole day by the time the clock struck nine, and released them; whilst her pupil, who never was cross long together, took a hop, skip, and jump, to the dining-room, and was as fresh as ever in the eager hope that the post would bring a letter from home.

Lady Barbara read prayers in the dining-room at nine, and there breakfasted with Kate and Mrs. Lacy, sending up a tray to Lady Jane in her bed-room. Those were apt to be grave breakfasts; not like the merry mornings at home, when chatter used to go on in half whispers between the younger ones, with laughs, breaking out in sudden gusts, till a little over-loudness brought one of Mary's good-natured "Hushes," usually answered with, "O Mary, such fun!"

It was Lady Barbara's time for asking about all the lessons of the day before; and though these were usually fairly done, and Mrs. Lacy was always a kind reporter, it was rather awful; and what was worse, were the strictures on deportment. For it must be confessed, that Lady Caergwent, though neatly and prettily made, with delicate little feet and hands, and a strong upright back, was a remarkably awkward child; and the more she was lectured, the more ungraceful she made herself--partly from thinking about it, and from fright making her abrupt, partly from being provoked. She had never been so ungainly at Oldburgh; she never was half so awkward in the school-room, as she would be while taking her cup of tea from Lady Barbara, or handing the butter to her governess. And was it not wretched to be ordered to do it again, and again, and again, (each time worse than the last--the fingers more crooked, the elbow more stuck out, the shoulder more forward than before), when there was a letter in Sylvia's writing lying on the table unopened?

And whereas it had been the fashion at St. James's Parsonage to compare Kate's handing her plate to a chimpanzee asking for nuts, it was hard that in Bruton Street these manners should be attributed to the barbarous country in which she had grown up! But that, though Kate did not know it, was very much her own fault. She could never be found fault with but she answered again. She had been scarcely broken of replying and justifying herself, even to Mr. Wardour, and had often argued with Mary till he came in and put a sudden sharp stop to it; and now she usually defended herself with "Papa says--" or "Mary says--" and though she really thought she spoke the truth, she made them say such odd things, that it was no wonder Lady Barbara thought they had very queer notions of education, and that her niece had nothing to do but to unlearn their lessons. Thus:

"Katharine, easy-chairs were not meant for little girls to lounge in."

"Oh, Papa says he doesn't want one always to sit upright and stupid."

So Lady Barbara was left to suppose that Mr. Wardour's model attitude for young ladies was sitting upon one leg in an easy-chair, with the other foot dangling, the forehead against the back, and the arm of the chair used as a desk! How was she to know that this only meant that he had once had the misfortune to express his disapproval of the high-backed long-legged school-room chairs formerly in fashion? In fact, Kate could hardly be forbidden anything without her replying that Papa or Mary ALWAYS let her do it; till at last she was ordered, very decidedly, never again to quote Mr. and Miss Wardour, and especially not to call him Papa.

Kate's eyes flashed at this; and she was so angry, that no words would come but a passionate stammering "I can't--I can't leave off; I won't!"

Lady Barbara looked stern and grave. "You must be taught what is suitable to your position, Lady Caergwent; and until you have learnt to feel it yourself, I shall request Mrs. Lacy to give you an additional lesson every time you call Mr. Wardour by that name."

Aunt Barbara's low slow way of speaking when in great displeasure was a terrific thing, and so was the set look of her handsome mouth and eyes. Kate burst into a violent fit of crying, and was sent away in dire disgrace. When she had spent her tears and sobs, she began to think over her aunt's cruelty and ingratitude, and the wickedness of trying to make her ungrateful too; and she composed a thrilling speech, as she called it--"Lady Barbara Umfraville, when the orphan was poor and neglected, my Uncle Wardour was a true father to me. You may tear me with wild horses ere I will cease to give him the title of--No; and I will call him papa--no, father--with my last breath!"

What the countess might have done if Lady Barbara had torn her with wild horses must remain uncertain. It is quite certain that the mere fixing of those great dark eyes was sufficient to cut off Pa--at its first syllable, and turn it into a faltering "my uncle;" and that, though Kate's heart was very sore and angry, she never, except once or twice when the word slipped out by chance, incurred the penalty, though she would have respected herself more if she had been brave enough to bear something for the sake of showing her love to Mr. Wardour.

And the fact was, that self-justification and carelessness of exact correctness of truth had brought all this upon her, and given her aunt this bad opinion of her friends!

But this is going a long way from the description of Kate's days in Bruton Street.

After breakfast, she was sent out with Mrs. Lacy for a walk. If she had a letter from home, she read it while Josephine dressed her as if she had been a doll; or else she had a story book in hand, and was usually lost in it when Mrs. Lacy looked into her room to see if she were ready.

To walk along the dull street, and pace round and round the gardens in Berkeley Square, was not so entertaining as morning games in the garden with Sylvia;

and these were times of feeling very like a prisoner. Other children in the gardens seemed to be friends, and played together; but this the aunts had forbidden her, and she could only look on, and think of Sylvia and Charlie, and feel as if one real game of play would do her all the good in the world.

To be sure she could talk to Mrs. Lacy, and tell her about Sylvia, and deliver opinions upon the characters in her histories and stories; but it often happened that the low grave "Yes, my dear," showed by the very tone that her governess had heard not a word; and at the best, it was dreary work to look up and discourse to nothing but the black crape veil that Mrs. Lacy always kept down.

"I cannot think why I should have a governess in affliction; it is very hard upon me!" said Kate to herself.

Why did she never bethink herself how hard the afflictions were upon Mrs. Lacy, and what good it would have done her if her pupil had tried to be like a gentle little daughter to her, instead of merely striving for all the fun she could get?

The lesson time followed. Kate first repeated what she had learnt the day before; and then had a French master two days in the week; on two more, one for arithmetic and geography; and on the other two, a drawing master. She liked these lessons, and did well in all, as soon as she left off citing Mary Wardour's pronunciations, and ways of doing sums. Indeed, she had more lively conversation with her French master, who was a very good-natured old man, than with anyone else, except Josephine; and she liked writing French letters for him to correct, making them be from the imaginary little girls whom she was so fond of drawing, and sending them to Sylvia.

After the master was gone, Kate prepared for him for the next day, and did a little Italian reading with Mrs. Lacy; after which followed reading of history, and needle-work. Lady Barbara was very particular that she should learn to work well, and was a good deal shocked at her very poor performances. "She had thought that plain needle-work, at least, would be taught in a clergyman's family."

"Mary tried to teach me; but she says all my fingers are thumbs."

And so poor Mrs. Lacy found them.

Mrs. Lacy and her pupil dined at the ladies' luncheon; and this was pleasanter than the breakfast, from the presence of Aunt Jane, whose kiss of greeting was a comforting cheering moment, and who always was so much distressed and hurt at the sight of her sister's displeasure, that Aunt Barbara seldom reproved before her. She always had a kind word to say; Mrs. Lacy seemed brighter and less oppressed in the sound of her voice; everyone was more at ease; and when speaking to her, or waiting upon her, Lady Barbara was no longer stern in manner nor dry in voice. The meal was not lively; there was nothing like the talk about parish matters, nor the jokes that she was used to; and though she was helped first, and ceremoniously waited on, she might not speak unless she was spoken to; and was it not very cruel, first to make everything so dull that no one could help yawning, and then to treat a yawn as a dire offence?

The length of the luncheon was a great infliction, because all the time from that to three o'clock was her own. It was a poor remnant of the entire afternoons which she and Sylvia had usually disposed of much as they pleased; and even what there was of it, was not to be spent in the way for which the young limbs longed. No one was likely to play at blind man's buff and hare and hounds in that house; and even her poor attempt at throwing her gloves or a pen-wiper against the wall, and catching them in the rebound, and her scampers up- stairs two steps at once, and runs down with a leap down the last four steps, were summarily stopped, as un-ladylike, and too noisy for Aunt Jane. Kate did get a private run and leap whenever she could, but never with a safe conscience; and that spoilt the pleasure, or made it guilty and alarmed.

All she could do really in peace was reading or drawing, or writing letters to Sylvia. Nobody had interfered with any of these occupations, though Kate knew that none of them were perfectly agreeable to Aunt Barbara, who had been heard to speak of children's reading far too many silly story-books now-a-days, and had declared that the child would cramp her hand for writing or good drawing with that nonsense.

However, Lady Jane had several times submitted most complacently to have a whole long history in pictures explained to her, smiling very kindly, but not apparently much the wiser. And one, at least, of the old visions of wealth was fulfilled, for Kate's pocket-money enabled her to keep herself in story-books and unlimited white paper, as well as to set up a paint-box with real good colours. But somehow, a new tale every week had not half the zest that stories had when a fresh book only came into the house by rare and much prized chances; and though the paper was smooth, and the blue and red lovely, it was not half so nice to draw and paint as with Sylvia helping, and the remains of Mary's rubbings for making illuminations; nay, Lily spoiling everything, and Armyn and Charlie laughing at her were now remembered as ingredients in her pleasure; and she would hardly have had the heart to go on drawing but that she could still send her pictorial stories to Sylvia, and receive remarks on them. There were no more Lady Ethelindas in flounces in Kate's drawings now; her heroines were always clergymen's daughters, or those of colonists cutting down trees and making the butter.

At three o'clock the carriage came to the door; and on Mondays and Thursdays took Lady Caergwent and her governess to a mistress who taught dancing and cal-isthenic exercises, and to whom her aunts trusted to make her a little more like a countess than she was at present. Those were poor Kate's black days of the week; when her feet were pinched, and her arms turned the wrong way, as it seemed to her; and she was in perpetual disgrace. And oh, that polite disgrace! Those wishes that her Ladyship would assume a more aristocratic deportment, were so infinitely worse than a good scolding! Nothing could make it more dreadful, except Aunt Barbara's coming in at the end to see how she was getting on.

The aunts, when Lady Jane was well enough, used to take their drive while the dancing lesson was in progress, and send the carriage afterwards to bring their niece home. On the other days of the week, when it was fine, the carriage set Mrs. Lacy and Kate down in Hyde Park for their walk, while the aunts drove about; and this, after the first novelty, was nearly as dull as the morning walk. The quiet decorous pacing along was very tiresome after skipping in the lanes at home; and once, when Mrs. Lacy had let her run freely in Kensington Gardens, Lady Barbara was much displeased with her, and said Lady Caergwent was too old for such habits.

There was no sight-seeing. Kate had told Lady Jane how much she wished to see the Zoological Gardens and British Museum, and had been answered that some day when she was very good Aunt Barbara would take her there; but the day never came, though whenever Kate had been in no particular scrape for a little while, she hoped it was coming. Though certainly days without scrapes were not many: the loud tones, the screams of laughing that betrayed her undignified play with Jose-phine, the attitudes, the skipping and jumping like the gambols of a calf, the won-derful tendency of her clothes to get into mischief--all were continually bringing trouble upon her.

If a splash of mud was in the street, it always came on her stockings; her meals left reminiscences on all her newest dresses; her hat was always blowing off; and her skirts curiously entangled themselves in rails and balusters, caught upon nails, and tore into ribbons; and though all the repairs fell to Josephine's lot, and the purchase of new garments was no such difficulty as of old, Aunt Barbara was even more severe on such mishaps than Mary, who had all the trouble and expense of them.

After the walk, Kate had lessons to learn for the next day--poetry, dates, grammar, and the like; and after them came her tea; and then her evening toilette, when, as the aunts were out of hearing, she refreshed herself with play and chatter with Josephine. She was supposed to talk French to her; but it was very odd sort of French, and Josephine did not insist on its being better. She was very good- natured, and thought "Miladi" had a dull life; so she allowed a good many things that a more thoughtful person would have known to be inconsistent with obedience to Lady Barbara.

When dressed, Kate had to descend to the drawing-room, and there await her aunts coming up from dinner. She generally had a book of her own, or else she read bits of those lying on the tables, till Lady Barbara caught her, and in spite of her protest that at home she might always read any book on the table ordered her never to touch any without express permission.

Sometimes the aunts worked; sometimes Lady Barbara played and sang. They wanted Kate to sit up as they did with fancy work, and she had a bunch of flowers in Berlin wool which she was supposed to be grounding; but she much disliked it, and seldom set three stitches when her aunts' eyes were not upon her. Lady Jane was a great worker, and tried to teach her some pretty stitches; but though she began by liking to sit by the soft gentle aunt, she was so clumsy a pupil, that Lady Barbara declared that her sister must not be worried, and put a stop to the lessons. So Kate sometimes read, or dawdled over her grounding; or when Aunt Barbara was singing, she would nestle up to her other aunt, and go off into some dreamy fancy of growing up, getting home to the Wardours, or having them to live with her at her own home; or even of a great revolution, in which, after the pattern of the French nobility, she should have to maintain Aunt Jane by the labour of her hands! What was to become of Aunt Barbara was uncertain; perhaps she was to be in prison, and

Kate to bring food to her in a little basket every day; or else she was to run away: but Aunt Jane was to live in a nice little lodging, with no one to wait on her but her dear little niece, who was to paint beautiful screens for her livelihood, and make her coffee with her own hands. Poor Lady Jane!

Bed-time came at last--horrible bed-time, with all its terrors! At first Kate persuaded Josephine and her light to stay till sleep came to put an end to them; but Lady Barbara came up one evening, declared that a girl of eleven years old must not be permitted in such childish nonsense, and ordered Josephine to go down at once, and always to put out the candle as soon as Lady Caergwent was in bed.

Lady Barbara would hardly have done so if she had known how much suffering she caused; but she had always been too sensible to know what the misery of fancies could be, nor how the silly little brain imagined everything possible and impossible; sometimes that thieves were breaking in--sometimes that the house was on fire--sometimes that she should be smothered with pillows, like the princes in the Tower, for the sake of her title--sometimes that the Gunpowder Plot would be acted under the house!

Most often of all it was a thought that was not foolish and unreal like the rest. It was the thought that the Last Judgment might be about to begin. But Kate did not use that thought as it was meant to be used when we are bidden to "watch." If she had done so, she would have striven every morning to "live this day as if the last." But she never thought of it in the morning, nor made it a guide to her actions; or else she would have dreaded it less. And at night it did not make her particular about obedience. It only made her want to keep Josephine; as if Josephine and a candle could protect her from that Day and Hour! And if the moment had come, would she not have been safer trying to endure hardness for the sake of obedience--with the holy verses Mr. Wardour had taught her on her lips, alone with her God and her good angel--than trying to forget all in idle chatter with her maid, and contrary to known commands, detaining her by foolish excuses?

It is true that Kate did not feel as if obedience to Lady Barbara was the same duty as obedience to "Papa." Perhaps it was not in the nature of things that she should; but no one can habitually practise petty disobedience to one "placed in authority over" her, without hurting the whole disposition.

CHAPTER IV.

Thursday morning! Bother--calisthenic day!--I'll go to sleep again, to put it off as long as I can. If I was only a little countess in her own feudal keep, I would get up in the dawn, and gather flowers in the May dew--primroses and eglantine!--Charlie says it is affected to call sweet-briar eglantine.--Sylvia! Sylvia! that thorn has got hold of me; and there's Aunt Barbara coming down the lane in the baker's jiggeting cart.--Oh dear! was it only dreaming? I thought I was gathering dog-roses with Charlie and Sylvia in the lane; and now it is only Thursday, and horrid calisthenic day! I suppose I must wake up.

'Awake, my soul, and with the sun Thy daily stage of duty run.'

I'm sure it's a very tiresome sort of stage! We used to say, 'As happy as a queen:' I am sure if the Queen is as much less happy than a countess as I am than a common little girl, she must be miserable indeed! It is like a rule-of-three sum. Let me see--if a common little girl has one hundred happinesses a day, and a countess only-- only five--how many has the Queen? No--but how much higher is a queen than a countess? If I were Queen, I would put an end to aunts and to calisthenic exercises; and I would send for all my orphan nobility, and let them choose their own governesses and playfellows, and always live with country clergymen! I am sure nobody ought to be oppressed as Aunt Barbara oppresses me: it is just like James V. of Scotland when the Douglases got hold of him! I wonder what is the use of being a countess, if one never is to do anything to please oneself, and one is to live with a cross old aunt!"

Most likely everyone is of Lady Caergwent's morning opinion--that Lady Barbara Umfraville was cross, and that it was a hard lot to live in subjection to her. But there are two sides to a question; and there were other hardships in that house besides those of the Countess of Caergwent.

Forty years ago, two little sisters had been growing up together, so fond of each other that they were like one; and though the youngest, Barbara, was always brighter, stronger, braver, and cleverer, than gentle Jane, she never enjoyed what her sister could not do; and neither of them ever wanted any amusement beyond quiet play with their dolls and puzzles, contrivances in pretty fancy works, and walks with their governess in trim gravel paths. They had two elder brothers and one younger; but they had never played out of doors with them, and had not run about or romped since they were almost babies; they would not have known how; and Jane was always sickly and feeble, and would have been very unhappy with loud or active ways.

As time passed on, Jane became more weakly and delicate while Barbara grew up very handsome, and full of life and spirit, but fonder of her sister than ever, and always coming home from her parties and gaieties, as if telling Jane about them was the best part of all.

At last, Lady Barbara was engaged to be married to a brother officer of her second brother, James; but just then poor Jane fell so ill, that the doctors said she could not live through the year. Barbara loved her sister far too well to think of marrying at such a time, and said she must attend to no one else. All that winter and spring she was nursing her sister day and night, watching over her, and quite keeping up the little spark of life, the doctors said, by her tender care. And though Lady Jane lived on day after day, she never grew so much better as to be fit to hear of the engagement and that if she recovered her sister would be separated from her; and so weeks went on, and still nothing could be done about the marriage.

As it turned out, this was the best thing that could have happened to Lady Barbara; for in the course of this time, it came to her father's knowledge that her brother and her lover had both behaved disgracefully, and that, if she had married, she must have led a very unhappy life. He caused the engagement to be broken off. She knew it was right, and made no complaint to anybody; but she always believed that it was her brother James who had been the tempter, who had led his friend astray; and from that time, though she was more devoted than ever to her sick sister, she was soft and bright to nobody else. She did not complain, but she thought that things had been very hard with her; and when people repine their troubles do not make them kinder, but the brave grow stern and the soft grow fretful.

All this had been over for nearly thirty years, and the brother and the friend had both been long dead. Lady Barbara was very anxious to do all that she thought right; and she was so wise and sensible, and so careful of her sister Jane, that all the family respected her and looked up to her. She thought she had quite forgiven all that had passed: she did not know why it was so hard to her to take any notice of her brother James's only son. Perhaps, if she had, she would have forced herself to try to be more warm and kind to him, and not have inflamed Lord Caergwent's displeasure when he married imprudently. Her sister Jane had never known all that had passed: she had been too ill to hear of it at the time; and it was not Lady Barbara's way to talk to other people of her own troubles. But Jane was always led by her sister, and never thought of people, or judged events, otherwise than as Barbara told her; so that, kind and gentle as she was by nature, she was like a double of her sister, instead of by her mildness telling on the family counsels. The other brother, Giles, had been aware of all, and saw how it was; but he was so much younger than the rest, that he was looked on by them like a boy long after he was grown up, and had not felt entitled to break through his sister Barbara's reserve, so as to venture on opening out the sorrows so long past, and pleading for his brother James's family, though he had done all he could for them himself. He had indeed been almost constantly on foreign service, and had seen very little of his sisters.

Since their father's death, the two sisters had lived their quiet life together. They were just rich enough to live in the way they thought the duty of persons in their rank, keeping their carriage for Lady Jane's daily drive, and spending two months every year by the sea, and one at Caergwent Castle with their eldest brother. They always had a spare room for any old friend who wanted to come up to town; and they did many acts of kindness, and gave a great deal to be spent on the poor of their parish. They did the same quiet things every day: one liked what the other liked; and Lady Barbara thought, morning, noon, and night, what would be good for her sister's health; while Lady Jane rested on Barbara's care, and was always pleased with whatever came in her way.

And so the two sisters had gone on year after year, and were very happy in their own way, till the great grief came of losing their eldest brother; and not long after him, his son, the nephew who had been their great pride and delight, and for whom they had so many plans and hopes.

And with his death, there came what they felt to be the duty and necessity of trying to fit the poor little heiress for her station. They were not fond of any children; and it upset all their ways very much to have to make room for a little girl, her maid, and her governess; but still, if she had been such a little girl as they had been, and always like the well-behaved children whom they saw in drawing-rooms, they would have known what kind of creature had come into their hands.

But was it not very hard on them that their niece should turn out a little wild harum-scarum creature, such as they had never dreamt of-- really unable to move without noises that startled Lady Jane's nerves, and threw Lady Barbara into despair at the harm they would do--a child whose untutored movements were a constant eye-sore and distress to them; and though she could sometimes be bright and fairy-like if unconstrained, always grew abrupt and uncouth when under restraint--a child very far from silly, but apt to say the silliest things--learning quickly all that was mere head-work, but hopelessly or obstinately dull at what was to be done by the fingers--a child whose ways could not be called vulgar, but would have been completely tom-boyish, except for a certain timidity that deprived them of the one merit of courage, and a certain frightened consciousness that was in truth modesty, though it did not look like it? To have such a being to endure, and more than that, to break into the habits of civilized life, and the dignity of a lady of rank, was no small burden for them; but they thought it right, and made up their minds to bear it.

Of course it would have been better if they had taken home the little orphan when she was destitute and an additional weight to Mr. Wardour; and had she been actually in poverty or distress, with no one to take care of her, Lady Barbara would have thought it a duty to provide for her: but knowing her to be in good hands, it had not then seemed needful to inflict the child on her sister, or to conquer her own distaste to all connected with her unhappy brother James. No one had ever thought of the little Katharine Aileve Umfraville becoming the head of the family; for then young Lord Umfraville was in his full health and strength.

And why DID Lady Barbara only now feel the charge of the child a duty? Perhaps it was because, without knowing it, she had been brought up to make an idol of the state and consequence of the earldom, since she thought breeding up the girl for a countess incumbent on her, when she had not felt tender compassion for the brother's orphan grandchild. So somewhat of the pomps of this world may have come in to blind her eyes; but whatever she did was because she thought it right to do, and when Kate thought of her as cross, it was a great mistake. Lady Barbara had great control of temper, and did everything by rule, keeping herself as strictly as she did everyone else except Lady Jane; and though she could not like such a troublesome little incomprehensible wild cat as Katharine, she was always trying to do her strict justice, and give her whatever in her view was good or useful.

But Kate esteemed it a great holiday, when, as sometimes happened, Aunt Barbara went out to spend the evening with some friends; and she, under promise of being very good, used to be Aunt Jane's companion.

Those were the times when her tongue took a holiday, and it must be confessed, rather to the astonishment and confusion of Lady Jane.

"Aunt Jane, do tell me about yourself when you were a little girl?"

"Ah! my dear, that does not seem so very long ago. Time passes very quickly. To think of such a great girl as you being poor James's grandchild!"

"Was my grandpapa much older than you, Aunt Jane?"

"Only three years older, my dear."

"Then do tell me how you played with him?"

"I never did, my dear; I played with your Aunt Barbara."

"Dear me how stupid! One can't do things without boys."

"No, my dear; boys always spoil girls' play, they are so rough."

"Oh! no, no, Aunt Jane; there's no fun unless one is rough--I mean, not rough exactly; but it's no use playing unless one makes a jolly good noise."

"My dear," said Lady Jane, greatly shocked, "I can't bear to hear you talk so, nor to use such words."

"Dear me, Aunt Jane, we say 'Jolly' twenty times a day at St. James's, and nobody minds."

"Ah! yes, you see you played with boys."

"But our boys are not rough, Aunt Jane," persisted Kate, who liked hearing herself talk much better than anyone else. "Mary says Charlie is a great deal less riotous than I am, especially since he went to school; and Armyn is too big to be riotous. Oh dear, I wish Mr. Brown would send Armyn to London; he said he would be sure to come and see me, and he is the jolliest, most delightful fellow in the world!"

"My dear child," said Lady Jane in her soft, distressed voice, "indeed that is not the way young ladies talk of--of--boys."

"Armyn is not a boy, Aunt Jane; he's a man. He is a clerk, you know, and will get a salary in another year."

"A clerk!"

"Yes; in Mr. Brown's office, you know. Aunt Jane, did you ever go out to tea?"

"Yes, my dear; sometimes we drank tea with our little friends in the dolls' tea-cups."

"Oh! you can't think what fun we have when Mrs. Brown asks us to tea. She has got the nicest garden in the world, and a greenhouse, and a great squirt-syringe, I mean, to water it; and we always used to get it, till once, without meaning it, I squirted right through the drawing-room window, and made such a puddle; and Mrs. Brown thought it was Charlie, only I ran in and told of myself, and Mrs. Brown said it was very generous, and gave me a Venetian weight with a little hermit in a snow-storm; only it is worn out now, and won't snow, so I gave it to little Lily when we had the whooping-cough."

By this time Lady Jane was utterly ignorant what the gabble was about, except that Katharine had been in very odd company, and done very strange things with those boys, and she gave a melancholy little sound in the pause; but Kate, taking breath, ran on again -

"It is because Mrs. Brown is not used to educating children, you know, that she fancies one wants a reward for telling the truth; I told her so, but Mary thought it would vex her, and stopped my mouth. Well, then we young ones--that is, Charlie, and Sylvia, and Armyn, and I--drank tea out on the lawn. Mary had to sit up and be company; but we had such fun! There was a great old laurel tree, and Armyn put Sylvia and me up into the fork; and that was our nest, and we were birds, and he fed us with strawberries; and we pretended to be learning to fly, and stood up flapping our frocks and squeaking, and Charlie came under and danced the branches about. We didn't like that; and Armyn said it was a shame, and hunted him away, racing all round the garden; and we scrambled down by ourselves, and came down on the slope. It is a long green slope, right down to the river, all smooth and turfy, you know; and I was standing at the top, when Charlie comes slyly, and saying he would help the little bird to fly, gave me one push, and down I went, roll, roll, tumble, tumble, till Sylvia REALLY thought she heard my neck crack! Wasn't it fun?"

"But the river, my dear!" said Lady Jane, shuddering.

"Oh! there was a good flat place before we came to the river, and I stopped long before that! So then, as we had been the birds of the air, we thought we would be the fishes of the sea; and it was nice and shallow, with dear little caddises and river cray-fish, and great British pearl-shells at the bottom. So we took off our shoes and stockings, and Charlie and Armyn turned up their trousers, and we had such a nice paddling. I really thought I should have got a British pearl then; and you know there were some in the breast-plate of Venus."

"In the river! Did your cousin allow that?"

"Oh yes; we had on our old blue checks; and Mary never minds anything when Armyn is there to take care of us. When they heard in the drawing-room what we had been doing, they made Mary sing 'Auld Lang Syne,' because of 'We twa hae paidlit in the burn frae morning sun till dine;' and whenever in future times I meet Armyn, I mean to say,

'We twa hae paidlit in the burn
Frae morning sun till dine;
We've wandered many a weary foot
Sin auld lang syne.'

Or perhaps I shall be able to sing it, and that will be still prettier."

And Kate sat still, thinking of the prettiness of the scene of the stranger, alone in the midst of numbers, in the splendid drawing- rooms, hearing the sweet voice of the lovely young countess at the piano, singing this touching memorial of the simple days of childhood.

Lady Jane meanwhile worked her embroidery, and thought what wonderful disadvantages the poor child had had, and that Barbara really must not be too severe on her, after she had lived with such odd people, and that it was very fortunate that she had been taken away from them before she had grown any older, or more used to them.

Soon after, Kate gave a specimen of her manners with boys. When she went into the dining-room at luncheon time one wet afternoon, she heard steps on the stairs behind her aunt's, and there appeared a very pleasant-looking gentleman, followed by a boy of about her own age.

"Here is our niece," said Lady Barbara. "Katharine, come and speak to Lord de la Poer."

Kate liked his looks, and the way in which he held out his hand to her; but she knew she should be scolded for her awkward greeting: so she put out her hand as if she had no use of her arm above the elbow, hung down her head, and said "--do;" at least no more was audible.

But there was something comfortable and encouraging in the grasp of the strong large hand over the foolish little fingers; and he quite gave them to his son, whose shake was a real treat; the contact with anything young was like meeting a follow-countryman in a foreign land, though neither as yet spoke.

She found out that the boy's name was Ernest, and that his father was taking him to school, but had come to arrange some business matters for her aunts upon the way. She listened with interest to Lord de la Poer's voice, for she liked it, and was sure he was a greater friend there than any she had before seen. He was talking about Giles--that was her uncle, the Colonel in India; and she first gathered from what was passing that her uncle's eldest and only surviving son, an officer in his own regiment, had never recovered a wound he had received at the relief of Lucknow, and that if he did not get better at Simlah, where his mother had just taken him, his father thought of retiring and bringing him home, though all agreed that it would be a very unfortunate thing that the Colonel should be obliged to resign his command before getting promoted; but they fully thought he would do so, for this was the last of his children; another son had been killed in the Mutiny, and two or three little girls had been born and died in India.

Kate had never known this. Her aunts never told her anything, nor talked over family affairs before her; and she was opening her ears most eagerly, and turning her quick bright eyes from one speaker to the other with such earnest attention, that the guest turned kindly to her, and said, "Do you remember your uncle?"

"Oh dear no! I was a little baby when he went away."

Kate never used DEAR as an adjective except at the beginning of a letter, but always, and very unnecessarily, as an interjection; and this time it was so emphatic as to bring Lady Barbara's eyes on her.

"Did you see either Giles or poor Frank before they went out to him?"

"Oh dear no!"

This time the DEAR was from the confusion that made her always do the very thing she ought not to do.

"No; my niece has been too much separated from her own relations," said Lady Barbara, putting this as an excuse for the "Oh dears."

"I hope Mr. Wardour is quite well," said Lord de la Poer, turning again to Kate.

"Oh yes, quite, thank you;" and then with brightening eyes, she ventured on "Do you know him?"

"I saw him two or three times," he answered with increased kindness of manner. "Will you remember me to him when you write?"

"Very well," said Kate promptly; "but he says all those sort of things are nonsense."

The horror of the two aunts was only kept in check by the good manners that hindered a public scolding; but Lord de la Poer only laughed heartily, and said, "Indeed! What sort of things, may I ask, Lady Caergwent?"

"Why--love, and regards, and remembrances. Mary used to get letters from her school-fellows, all filled with dearest loves, and we always laughed at her; and Armyn used to say them by heart beforehand," said Kate.

"I beg to observe," was the answer, in the grave tone which, however, Kate understood as fun, "that I did not presume to send my love to Mr. Wardour. May not that make the case different?"

"Yes," said Kate meditatively; "only I don't know that your remembrance would be of more use than your love."

"And are we never to send any messages unless they are of use?" This was a puzzling question, and Kate did not immediately reply.

"None for pleasure--eh?"

"Well, but I don't see what would be the pleasure."

"What, do you consider it pleasurable to be universally forgotten?"

"Nobody ever could forget Pa--my Uncle Wardour," cried Kate, with eager vehemence flashing in her eyes.

"Certainly not," said Lord de la Poer, in a voice as if he were much pleased with her; "he is not a man to be forgotten. It is a privilege to have been brought up by him. But come, Lady Caergwent, since you are so critical, will you be pleased to devise some message for me, that may combine use, pleasure, and my deep respect for him?" and as she sat beside him at the table, he laid his hand on hers, so that she felt that he really meant what he said.

She sat fixed in deep thought; and her aunts, who had been miserable all through the conversation, began to speak of other things; but in the midst the shrill little voice broke in, "I know what!" and good- natured Lord de la Poer turned at once, smiling, and saying, "Well, what?"

"If you would help in the new aisle! You know the church is not big enough; there are so many people come into the district, with the new ironworks, you know; and we have not got half room enough, and can't make more, though we have three services; and we want to build a new aisle, and it will cost 250 pounds, but we have only got 139 pounds 15s. 6d. And if you would but be so kind as to give one sovereign for it--that would be better than remembrances and respects, and all that sort of thing."

"I rather think it would," said Lord de la Poer; and though Lady Barbara eagerly exclaimed, "Oh! do not think of it; the child does not know what she is talking of. Pray excuse her--" he took out his purse, and from it came a crackling smooth five-pound note, which he put into the hand, saying, "There, my dear, cut that in two, and send the two halves on different days to Mr. Wardour, with my best wishes for his success in his good works. Will that do?"

Kate turned quite red, and only perpetrated a choked sound of her favourite -q. For the whole world she could not have said more: but though she knew perfectly well that anger and wrath were hanging over her, she felt happier than for many a long week.

Presently the aunts rose, and Lady Barbara said to her in the low ceremonious voice that was a sure sign of warning and displeasure, "You had better come up stairs with us, Katharine, and amuse Lord Ernest in the back drawing-room while his father is engaged with us."

Kate's heart leapt up at the sound "amuse." She popped her precious note into her pocket, bounded up-stairs, and opened the back drawing- room door for her playfellow, as he brought up the rear of the procession.

Lord de la Poer and Lady Barbara spread the table with papers; Lady Jane sat by; the children were behind the heavy red curtains that parted off the second room. There was a great silence at first, then began a little tittering, then a little chattering, then presently a stifled explosion. Lady Barbara began to betray some restlessness; she really must see what that child was about.

"No, no," said Lord de la Poer; "leave them in peace. That poor girl will never thrive unless you let her use her voice and limbs. I shall make her come over and enjoy herself with my flock when we come up en masse."

The explosions were less carefully stifled, and there were some sounds of rushing about, some small shrieks, and then the door shut, and there was a silence again.

By this it may be perceived that Kate and Ernest had become tolerably intimate friends. They had informed each other of what games were their favourites; Kate had told him the Wardour names and ages; and required from him in return those of his brothers and sisters. She had been greatly delighted by learning that Adelaide was no end of a hand at climbing trees; and that whenever she should come and stay at their house, Ernest would teach her to ride. And then they began to consider what play was possible under the present circumstances-- beginning they hardly knew how, by dodging one another round and round the table, making snatches at one another, gradually assuming the characters of hunter and Red Indian. Only when the hunter had snatched up Aunt Jane's tortoise-shell paper-cutter to stab with, complaining direfully that it was a stupid place, with nothing for a gun, and the Red Indian's crinoline had knocked down two chairs, she recollected the consequences in time to strangle her own war-whoop, and suggested that they should be safer on the stairs; to which Ernest readily responded, adding that there was a great gallery at home all full of pillars and statues, the jolliest place in the world for making a row.

"Oh dear! oh dear! how I hope I shall go there!" cried Kate, swinging between the rails of the landing-place. "I do want of all things to see a statue."

"A statue! why, don't you see lots every day?"

"Oh! I don't mean great equestrian things like the Trafalgar Square ones, or the Duke--or anything big and horrid, like Achilles in the Park, holding up a shield like a green umbrella. I want to see the work of the great sculptor Julio Romano."

"He wasn't a sculptor."

"Yes, he was; didn't he sculp--no, what is the word--Hermione. No; I mean they pretended he had done her."

"Hermione! What, have you seen the 'Winter's Tale?'"

"Papa--Uncle Wardour, that is--read it to us last Christmas."

"Well, I've seen it. Alfred and I went to it last spring with our tutor."

"Oh! then do, pray, let us play at it. Look, there's a little stand up there, where I have always so wanted to get up and be Hermione, and descend to the sound of slow music. There's a musical-box in the back drawing-room that will make the music."

"Very well; but I must be the lion and bear killing the courtier."

"O yes--very well, and I'll be courtier; only I must get a sofa- cushion to be Perdita."

"And where's Bohemia?"

"Oh! the hall must be Bohemia, and the stair-carpet the sea, because then the aunts won't hear the lion and bear roaring."

With these precautions, the characteristic roaring and growling of lion and bear, and the shrieks of the courtier, though not absolutely unheard in the drawing-room, produced no immediate results. But in the very midst of Lady Jane's signing her name to some paper, she gave a violent start, and dropped the pen, for they were no stage shrieks--"Ah! ah! It is coming down! Help me down! Ernest, Ernest! help me down! Ah!"--and then a great fall.

The little mahogany bracket on the wall had been mounted by the help of a chair, but it was only fixed into the plaster, being intended to hold a small lamp, and not for young ladies to stand on; so no sooner was the chair removed by which Kate had mounted, than she felt not only giddy in her elevation, but found her pedestal loosening! There was no room to jump; and Ernest, perhaps enjoying what he regarded as a girl's foolish fright, was a good way off, endeavouring to wind up the musical-box, when the bracket gave way, and Hermione descended precipitately with anything but the sound of soft music; and as the inhabitants of the drawing-room rushed out to the rescue, her legs were seen kicking in the air upon the landing-place; Ernest looking on, not knowing whether to laugh or be dismayed.

Lord de la Poer picked her up, and sat down on the stairs with her between his knees to look her over and see whether she were hurt, or what was the matter, while she stood half sobbing with the fright and shock. He asked his son rather severely what he had been doing to her.

"He did nothing," gasped Kate; "I was only Hermione."

"Yes, that's all, Papa," repeated Ernest; "it is all the fault of the plaster."

And a sort of explanation was performed between the two children, at which Lord de la Poer could hardly keep his gravity, though he was somewhat vexed at the turn affairs had taken. He was not entirely devoid of awe of the Lady Barbara, and would have liked his children to be on their best behaviour before her.

"Well," he said, "I am glad there is no worse harm done. You had better defer your statueship till we can find you a sounder pedestal, Lady Caergwent."

"Oh! call me Kate," whispered she in his ear, turning redder than the fright had made her.

He smiled, and patted her hand; then added, "We must go and beg pardon, I suppose; I should not wonder if the catastrophe had damaged Aunt Jane the most; and if so, I don't know what will be done to us!"

He was right; Lady Barbara had only satisfied herself that no bones had been broken, and then turned back to reassure her sister; but Lady Jane could not be frightened without suffering for it, and was lying back on the sofa, almost faint with palpitation, when Lord de la Poer, with Kate's hand in his, came to the door, looking much more consciously guilty than his son, who on the whole was more diverted than penitent at the commotion they had made.

Lady Barbara looked very grand and very dignified, but Lord de la Poer was so grieved for Lady Jane's indisposition, that she was somewhat softened; and then he began asking pardon, blending himself with the children so comically, that in all her fright and anxiety, Kate wondered how her aunt could help laughing.

It never was Lady Barbara's way to reprove before a guest; but this good gentleman was determined that she should not reserve her displeasure for his departure, and he would not go away till he had absolutely made her promise that his little friend, as he called Kate, should hear nothing more about anything that had that day taken place.

Lady Barbara kept her promise. She uttered no reproof either on her niece's awkward greeting, her abrupt conversation and its tendency to pertness, nor on the loudness of the unlucky game and the impropriety of climbing; nor even on what had greatly annoyed her, the asking for the subscription to the church. There was neither blame nor punishment; but she could not help a certain cold restraint of manner, by which Kate knew that she was greatly displeased, and regarded her as the most hopeless little saucy romp that ever maiden aunt was afflicted with.

And certainly it was hard on her. She had a great regard for Lord de la Poer, and thought his a particularly well trained family; and she was especially desirous that her little niece should appear to advantage before him. Nothing, she was sure, but Katharine's innate naughtiness could have made that well-behaved little Ernest break out into rudeness; and though his father had shown such good nature, he must have been very much shocked. What was to be done to tame this terrible little savage, was poor Lady Barbara's haunting thought, morning, noon, and night!

And what was it that Kate did want? I believe nothing could have made her perfectly happy, or suited to her aunt; but that she would have been infinitely happier and better off had she had the spirit of obedience, of humility, or of unselfishness.

CHAPTER V.

The one hour of play with Ernest de la Poer had the effect of making Kate long more and more for a return of "fun," and of intercourse with beings of her own age and of high spirits.

She wove to herself dreams of possible delights with Sylvia and Charlie, if the summer visit could be paid to them; and at other times she imagined her Uncle Giles's two daughters still alive, and sent home for education, arranging in her busy brain wonderful scenes, in which she, with their assistance, should be happy in spite of Aunt Barbara.

These fancies, however, would be checked by the recollection, that it was shocking to lower two happy spirits in Heaven into playful little girls upon earth; and she took refuge in the thought of the coming chance of playfellows, when Lord de la Poer was to bring his family to London. She had learnt the names and ages of all the ten; and even had her own theories as to what her contemporaries were to be like--Mary and Fanny, Ernest's elders, and Adelaide and Grace, who came next below him; she had a vision for each of them, and felt as if she already knew them.

Meanwhile, the want of the amount of air and running about to which she had been used, did really tell upon her; she had giddy feelings in the morning, tired limbs, and a weary listless air, and fretted over her lessons at times. So they showed her to the doctor, who came to see Lady Jane every alternate day; and when he said she wanted more exercise, her morning walk was made an hour longer, and a shuttlecock and battledores were bought, with which it was decreed that Mrs. Lacy should play with her for exactly half an hour every afternoon, or an hour when it was too wet to go out.

It must be confessed that this was a harder task to both than the music lessons. Whether it were from the difference of height, or from Kate's innate unhandiness, they never could keep that unhappy shuttlecock up more than three times; and Mrs. Lacy looked as grave and melancholy all the time as if she played it for a punishment, making little efforts to be cheerful that were sad to see. Kate hated it, and was always cross; and willingly would they have given it up by mutual consent, but the instant the tap of the cork against the parchment ceased, if it were not half-past five, down sailed Lady Barbara to inquire after her prescription.

She had been a famous battledore-player in the galleries of Caergwent Castle; and once when she took up the battledore to give a lesson, it seemed as if, between her and Mrs. Lacy, the shuttlecock would not come down--they kept up five hundred and eighty-one, and then only stopped because it was necessary for her to go to dinner.

She could not conceive anyone being unable to play at battledore, and thought Kate's failures and dislike pure perverseness. Once Kate by accident knocked her shuttlecock through the window, and hoped she had got rid of it; but she was treated as if she had done it out of naughtiness, and a new instrument of torture, as she called it, was bought for her.

It was no wonder she did not see the real care for her welfare, and thought this intensely cruel and unkind; but it was a great pity that she visited her vexation on poor Mrs. Lacy, to whom the game was even a greater penance than to herself, especially on a warm day, with a bad headache.

Even in her best days at home, Kate had resisted learning to take thought for others. She had not been considerate of Mary's toil, nor of Mr. Wardour's peace, except when Armyn or Sylvia reminded her; and now that she had neither of them to put it into her mind, she never once thought of her governess as one who ought to be spared and pitied. Yet if she had been sorry for Mrs. Lacy, and tried to spare her trouble and annoyance, how much irritability and peevishness, and sense of constant naughtiness, would have been prevented! And it was that feeling of being always naughty that was what had become the real dreariness of Kate's present home, and was far worse than the music, the battledore, or even the absence of fun.

At last came a message that Lady Caergwent was to be dressed for going out to make a call with Lady Barbara as soon as luncheon was over.

It could be on no one but the De la Poers; and Kate was so delighted, that she executed all manner of little happy hops, skips, and fidgets, all the time of her toilette, and caused many an expostulation of "Mais, Miladi!" from Josephine, before the pretty delicate blue and white muslin, worked white jacket, and white ribboned and feathered hat, were adjusted. Lady Barbara kept her little countess very prettily and quietly dressed; but it was at the cost of infinite worry of herself, Kate, and Josephine, for there never was a child whom it was so hard to keep in decent trim. Armyn's old saying, that she ought to be always kept dressed in sacking, as the only thing she could not spoil, was a true one; for the sharp hasty movements, and entire disregard of where she stepped, were so ruinous, that it was on the records of the Bruton Street household, that she had gone far to demolish eight frocks in ten days.

However, on this occasion she did get safe down to the carriage-- clothes, gloves, and all, without detriment or scolding; and jumped in first. She was a long way yet from knowing that, though her aunts gave the first place to her rank, it would have been proper in her to yield it to their years, and make way for them.

She was too childish to have learnt this as a matter of good breeding, but she might have learnt it of a certain parable, which she could say from beginning to end, that she should "sit not down in the highest room."

Her aunt sat down beside her, and spent the first ten minutes of the drive in enjoining on her proper behaviour at Lady de la Poer's. The children there were exceedingly well brought up, she said, and she was very desirous they should be her niece's friends; but she was certain that Lady de la Poer would allow no one to associate with them who did not behave properly.

"Lord de la Poer was very kind to me just as I was," said Kate, in her spirit of contradiction, which was always reckless of consequences.

"Gentlemen are no judges of what is becoming to a little girl," said Lady Barbara severely. "Unless you make a very different impression upon Lady de la Poer, she will never permit you to be the friend of her daughters."

"I wonder how I am to make an impression," meditated Kate, as they drove on; "I suppose it would make an impression if I stood up and repeated, 'Ruin seize thee, ruthless king!' or something of that sort, as soon as I got in. But one couldn't do that; and I am afraid nothing will happen. If the horses would only upset us at the door, and Aunt Barbara be nicely insensible, and the young countess show the utmost presence of mind! But nothing nice and like a book ever does happen. And after all, I believe that it is all nonsense about making impressions. Thinking of

them is all affectation; and one ought to be as simple and unconscious as one can."
A conclusion which did honour to the countess's sense. In fact, she had plenty of
sense, if only she had ever used it for herself, instead of for the little ladies she drew
on her quires of paper.

Lady Barbara had started early, as she really wished to find her friends at home;
and accordingly, when the stairs were mounted, and the aunt and niece were ush-
ered into a pretty bright-looking drawing- room, there they found all that were not
at school enjoying their after-dinner hour of liberty with their father and mother.

Lord de la Poer himself had the youngest in his arms, and looked very much
as if he had only just scrambled up from the floor; his wife was really sitting on the
ground, helping two little ones to put up a puzzle of wild beasts; and there was a little herd of girls at the farther corner, all very busy over something, towards which
Kate's longing eyes at once turned--even in the midst of Lord de la Poer's very kind
greeting, and his wife's no less friendly welcome.

It was true that, as Lady Barbara had said, they were all exceedingly well-bred
children. Even the little fellow in his father's arms, though but eighteen months
old, made no objection to hold out his fat hand graciously, and showed no shyness
when Lady Barbara kissed him! and the others all waited quietly over their several
occupations, neither shrinking foolishly from notice, nor putting themselves forward to claim it. Only the four sisters came up, and took their own special visitor
into the midst of them as their own property; the elder of them, however, at a sign
from her mamma, taking the baby in her arms, and carrying him off, followed by
the other two small ones- -only pausing at the door for him to kiss his little hand,
and wave it in the prettiest fashion of baby stateliness.

The other sisters drew Kate back with them into the room, where they had
been busy. Generally, however much she and Sylvia might wish it, they had found
acquaintance with other children absolutely impossible in the presence of grown-
up people, whose eyes and voices seemed to strike all parties dumb. But these children seemed in no wise constrained: one of them said at once, "We are so glad you
are come. Mamma said she thought you would before we went out, one of those
days."

"Isn't it horrid going out in London?" asked Kate, at once set at ease.

"It is not so nice as it is at home," said one of the girls; laughing; "except when it is our turn to go out with Mamma."

"She takes us all out in turn," explained another, "from Fanny, down to little Cecil the baby--and that is our great time for talking to her, when one has her all alone."

"And does she never take you out in the country?"

"Oh yes! but there are people staying with us then, or else she goes out with Papa. It is not a regular drive every day, as it is here."

Kate would not have had a drive with Aunt Barbara every day, for more than she could well say. However, she was discreet enough not to say so, and asked what they did on other days.

"Oh, we walk with Miss Oswald in the park, and she tells us stories, or we make them. We don't tell stories in the country, unless we have to walk straight along the drives, that, as Papa says, we may have some solace."

Then it was explained that Miss Oswald was their governess, and that they were very busy preparing for her birth-day. They were making a paper-case for her, all themselves, and this hour was their only time for doing it out of her sight in secret.

"But why do you make it yourselves?" said Kate; "one can buy such beauties at the bazaars."

"Yes; but Mamma says a present one has taken pains to make, is worth a great deal more than what is only bought; for trouble goes for more than money."

"But one can make nothing but nasty tumble-to-pieces things," objected Kate.

"That depends," said Lady Mary, in a very odd merry voice; and the other two, Adelaide and Grace, who were far too much alike for Kate to guess which was which, began in a rather offended manner to assure her that THEIR paper-case was to be anything but tumble-to-pieces. Fanny was to bind it, and Papa had promised to paste its back and press it.

"And Mamma drove with me to Richmond, on purpose to get leaves to spatter," added the other sister.

Then they showed Kate--whose eyes brightened at anything approaching to a mess--that they had a piece of coloured cardboard, on which leaves, chiefly fern, were pinned tightly down, and that the entire sheet was then covered with a spattering of ink from a tooth-brush drawn along the tooth of a comb. When the process was completed, the form of the loaf remained in the primitive colour of the card, thrown out by the cloud of ink-spots, and only requiring a tracing of its veins by a pen.

A space had been cleared for these operations on a side-table; and in spite of the newspaper, on which the appliances were laid, and even the comb and brush, there was no look of disarrangement or untidiness.

"Oh, do--do show me how you do it!" cried Kate, who had had nothing to do for months, with the dear delight of making a mess, except what she could contrive with her paints.

And Lady Grace resumed a brown-holland apron and bib, and opening her hands with a laugh, showed their black insides, then took up her implements.

"Oh, do--do let me try," was Kate's next cry; "one little bit to show Sylvia Wardour."

With one voice the three sisters protested that she had better not; she was not properly equipped, and would ink herself all over. If she would pin down a leaf upon the scrap she held up, Grace should spatter it for her, and they would make it up into anything she liked.

But this did not satisfy Kate at all; the pinning out of the leaf was stupid work compared with the glory of making the ink fly. In vain did Adelaide represent that all the taste and skill was in the laying out the leaves, and pinning them down, and that anyone could put on the ink; in vain did Mary represent the dirtiness of the work: this was the beauty of it in her eyes; and the sight of the black dashes sputtering through the comb filled her with emulation; so that she entreated, almost piteously, to be allowed to "do" an ivy loaf, which she had hastily, and not very carefully, pinned out with Mary's assistance--that is, she had feebly and unsteadily stuck every pin, and Mary had steadied them.

The new friends consented, seeing how much she was set on it; but Fanny, who had returned from the nursery, insisted on precautions-- took off the jacket, turned up the frock sleeves, and tied on an apron; though Kate fidgeted all the time, as if a great injury were being inflicted on her; and really, in her little frantic spirit, thought Lady Fanny a great torment, determined to delay her delight till her aunt should go away and put a stop to it.

When once she had the brush, she was full of fun and merriment, and kept her friends much amused by her droll talk, half to them, half to her work.

"There's a portentous cloud, isn't there? An inky cloud, if ever there was one! Take care, inhabitants below; growl, growl, there's the thunder; now comes the rain; hail, hail, all hail, like the beginning of Macbeth."

"Which the Frenchman said was in compliment to the climate," said Fanny; at which the whole company fell into convulsions of laughing; and neither Kate nor Grace exactly knew what hands or brush or comb were about; but whereas the little De La Poers had from their infancy laughed almost noiselessly, and without making faces, Kate for her misfortune had never been broken of a very queer contortion of her lips, and a cackle like a bantam hen's.

When this unlucky cackle had been several times repeated, it caused Lady Barbara, who had been sitting with her back to the inner room, to turn round.

Poor Lady Barbara! It would not be easy to describe her feelings when she saw the young lady, whom she had brought delicately blue and white, like a speedwell flower, nearly as black as a sweep.

Lord de la Poer broke out into an uncontrollable laugh, half at the aunt, half at the niece. "Why, she has grown a moustache!" he exclaimed. "Girls, what have you been doing to her?" and walking up to them, he turned Kate round to a mirror, where she beheld her own brown eyes looking out of a face dashed over with black specks, thicker about the mouth, giving her altogether much the colouring of a very dark man closely shaved. It was so exceedingly comical, that she went off into fits of laughing, in which she was heartily joined by all the merry party.

"There," said Lord de la Poer, "do you want to know what your Uncle Giles is like? you've only to look at yourself See, Barbara, is it not a capital likeness?"

"I never thought her like GILES," said her aunt gravely, with an emphasis on the name, as if she meant that the child did bear a likeness that was really painful to her.

"My dears," said the mother, "you should not have put her in such a condition; could you not have been more careful?"

Kate expected one of them to say, "She would do it in spite of us;" but instead of that Fanny only answered, "It is not so bad as it looks, Mamma; I believe her frock is quite safe; and we will soon have her face and hands clean."

Whereupon Kate turned round and said, "It is all my fault, and NOBODY'S

ELSE'S. They told me not, but it was such fun!"

And therewith she obeyed a pull from Grace, and ran upstairs with the party to be washed; and as the door shut behind them, Lord de la Poer said, "You need not be afraid of THAT likeness, Barbara. Whatever else she may have brought from her parsonage, she has brought the spirit of truth."

Though knowing that something awful hung over her head, Kate was all the more resolved to profit by her brief minutes of enjoyment; and the little maidens all went racing and flying along the passages together; Kate feeling as if the rapid motion among the other young feet was life once more.

"Well! your frock is all right; I hope your aunt will not be very angry with you," said Adelaide. (She know Adelaide now, for Grace was the inky one.)

"It is not a thing to be angry for," added Grace.

"No, it would not have been at my home," said Kate, with a sigh; "but, oh! I hope she will not keep me from coming here again."

"She shall not," exclaimed Adelaide; "Papa won't let her."

"She said your mamma would mind what your papa did not," said Kate, who was not very well informed on the nature of mammas.

"Oh, that's all stuff," decidedly cried Adelaide. "When Papa told us about you, she said, 'Poor child! I wish I had her here.'"

Prudent Fanny made an endeavour at chocking her little sister; but the light in Kate's eye, and the responsive face, drew Grace on to ask, "She didn't punish you, I hope, for your tumbling off the bracket?"

"No, your papa made her promise not; but she was very cross. Did he tell you about it?"

"Oh yes; and what do you think Ernest wrote? You must know he had grumbled excessively at Papa's having business with Lady Barbara; but his letter said, 'It wasn't at all slow at Lady Barbara's, for there was the jolliest fellow there you ever knew; mind you get her to play at acting.'"

Lady Fanny did not think this improving, and was very glad that the maid came in with hot water and towels, and put an end to it with the work of scrubbing.

Going home, Lady Barbara was as much displeased as Kate had expected, and with good reason. After all her pains, it was very strange that Katharine should be so utterly unfit to behave like a well-bred girl. There might have been excuse for her before she had been taught, but now it was mere obstinacy.

She should be careful how she took her out for a long time to come!

Kate's heart swelled within her. It was not obstinacy, she know; and that bit of injustice hindered her from seeing that it was really wilful recklessness. She was elated with Ernest's foolish school-boy account of her, which a more maidenly little girl would not have relished; she was strengthened in her notion that she was ill-used, by hearing that the De la Poers pitied her; and because she found that Aunt Barbara was considered to be a little wrong, she did not consider that she herself had ever been wrong at all.

And Lady Barbara was not far from the truth when she told her sister "that Katharine was perfectly hard and reckless; there was no such thing as making her sorry!"

CHAPTER VI.

After that first visit, Kate did see something of the De la Poers, but not more than enough to keep her in a constant ferment with the uncertain possibility, and the longing for the meetings.

The advances came from them; Lady Barbara said very truly, that she could not be responsible for making so naughty a child as her niece the companion of any well-regulated children; she was sure that their mother could not wish it, since nice and good as they naturally were, this unlucky Katharine seemed to infect them with her own spirit of riot and turbulence whenever they came near her.

There was no forwarding of the attempts to make appointments for walks in the Park, though really very little harm had ever come of them, guarded by the two governesses, and by Lady Fanny's decided ideas of propriety. That Kate embarked in long stories, and in their excitement raised her voice, was all that could be said against her on those occasions, and Mrs. Lacy forbore to say it.

Once, indeed, Kate was allowed to ask her friends to tea; but that proved a disastrous affair. Fanny was prevented from coming; and in the absence of her quiet elder-sisterly care, the spirits of Grace and Adelaide were so excited by Kate's drollery, that they were past all check from Mary, and drew her along with them into a state of frantic fun and mad pranks.

They were full of merriment all tea time, even in the presence of the two governesses; and when that was over, and Kate showed "the bracket," they began to grow almost ungovernable in their spirit of frolic and fun: they went into Kate's room, resolved upon being desert travellers, set up an umbrella hung round with cloaks for a tent, made camels of chairs, and finding those tardy, attempted riding on each other--with what results to Aunt Jane's ears below may be imagined--dressed up wild Arabs in bournouses of shawls, and made muskets of parasols, charging desperately, and shrieking for attack, defence, "for triumph or despair," as Kate observed, in one of her magnificent quotations. Finally, the endangered traveller, namely Grace, rushed down the stairs headlong, with the two Arabs clattering after him, banging with their muskets, and shouting their war-cry the whole height of the house.

The ladies in the drawing-room had borne a good deal; but Aunt Jane was by this time looking meekly distracted; and Lady Barbara sallying out, met the Arab Sheikh with his white frock over his head, descending the stairs in the rear, calling to his tribe in his sweet voice not to be so noisy--but not seeing before him through the said bournouse, he had very nearly struck Lady Barbara with his parasol before he saw her.

No one could be more courteous or full of apologies than the said Sheikh, who was in fact a good deal shocked at his unruly tribe, and quite acquiesced in the request that they would all come and sit quiet in the drawing-room, and play at some suitable game there.

It would have been a relief to Mary to have them thus disposed of safely; and Adelaide would have obeyed; but the other two had been worked up to a state of wildness, such as befalls little girls who have let themselves out of the control of their better sense.

They did not see why they should sit up stupid in the drawing-room; "Mary was as cross as Lady Barbara herself to propose it," said Grace, unfortunately just as the lady herself was on the stairs to enforce her desire, in her gravely courteous voice; whereupon Kate, half tired and wholly excited, burst out into a violent passionate fit of crying and sobbing, declaring that it was very hard, that whenever she had ever so little pleasure, Aunt Barbara always grudged it to her.

None of them had ever heard anything like it; to the little De la Poers she seemed like one beside herself, and Grace clung to Mary, and Adelaide to Miss Oswald, almost frightened at the screams and sobs that Kate really could not have stopped if she would. Lady Jane came to the head of the stairs, pale and trembling, begging to know who was hurt; and Mrs. Lacy tried gentle reasoning and persuading, but she might as well have spoken to the storm beating against the house.

Lady Barbara sternly ordered her off to her room; but the child did not stir-- indeed, she could not, except that she rocked herself to and fro in her paroxysms of sobbing, which seemed to get worse and worse every moment. It was Miss Oswald at last, who, being more used to little girls and their naughtiness than any of the others, saw the right moment at last, and said, as she knelt down by her, half kindly, half severely, "My dear, you had better let me take you up- stairs. I will help you: and you are only shocking everyone here."

Kate did let her take her up-stairs, though at every step there was a pause, a sob, a struggle; but a gentle hand on her shoulder, and firm persuasive voice in her ear, moved her gradually onwards, till the little pink room was gained; and there she threw herself on her bed in another agony of wild subs, unaware of Miss Oswald's parley at the door with Lady Barbara and Mrs. Lacy, and her entreaty that the patient might be left to her, which they were nothing loth to do.

When Kate recovered her speech, she poured out a wild and very naughty torrent, about being the most unhappy girl in the world; the aunts were always unkind to her; she never got any pleasure; she could not bear being a countess; she only wanted to go back to her old home, to Papa and Mary and Sylvia; and nobody would help her.

Miss Oswald treated the poor child almost as if she had been a little out of her mind, let her say it all between her sobs, and did not try to argue with her, but waited till the talking and the sobbing had fairly tried her out; and by that time the hour had come at which the little visitors were to go home. The governess rose up, and said she must go, asking in a quiet tone, as if all that had been said were mere mad folly, whether Lady Caergwent would come down with her, and tell her aunts she was sorry for the disturbance she had made.

Kate shrank from showing such a spectacle as her swollen, tear- stained, red-marbled visage. She was thoroughly sorry, and greatly ashamed; and she only gasped out, "I can't, I can't; don't let me see anyone."

"Then I will wish Mary and her sisters good-bye for you."

"Yes, please." Kate had no words for more of her sorrow and shame.

"And shall I say anything to your aunt for you?"

"I--I don't know; only don't let anyone come up."

"Then shall I tell Lady Barbara you are too much tired out now for talking, but that you will tell her in the morning how sorry you are?"

"Well, yes," said Kate rather grudgingly. "Oh, must you go?"

"I am afraid I must, my dear. Their mamma does not like Addie and Grace to be kept up later than their usual bed-time."

"I wish you could stay. I wish you were my governess," said Kate, clinging to her, and receiving her kind, friendly, pitying kiss.

And when the door had shut upon her, Kate's tears began to drop again at the thought that it was very hard that the little De la Poers, who had father, mother, and each other, should likewise have such a nice governess, while she had only poor sad dull Mrs. Lacy.

Had Kate only known what an unselfish little girl and Mrs. Lacy might have been to each other!

However, the first thing she could now think of was to avoid being seen or spoken to by anyone that night; and for this purpose she hastily undressed herself, bundled-up her hair as best she might, as in former days, said her prayers, and tumbled into bed, drawing the clothes over her head, resolved to give no sign of being awake, come who might.

Her shame was real, and very great. Such violent crying fits had overtaken her in past times, but had been thought to be outgrown. She well recollected the last. It was just after the death of her aunt, Mrs. Wardour, just when the strange stillness of sorrow in the house was beginning to lessen, and the children had forgotten themselves, and burst out into noise and merriment, till they grew unrestrained and quarrelsome; Charlie had offended Kate, she had struck him, and Mary coming on them, grieved and hurt at their conduct at such a time, had punished Kate for the blow, but missed perception of Charlie's offence; and the notion of injustice had caused the shrieking cries and violent sobs that had brought Mr. Wardour from the study in grave sorrowful severity.

What she had heard afterwards from him about not making poor Mary's task harder, and what she had heard from Mary about not paining him, had really restrained her; and she had thought such outbreaks passed by among the baby faults she had left behind, and was the more grieved and ashamed in consequence. She felt it a real exposure: she remembered her young friends' surprised and frightened eyes, and not only had no doubt their mother would really think her too naughty to be their playfellow, but almost wished that it might be so--she could never, never bear to see them again.

She heard the street door close after them, she heard the carriage drive away; she felt half relieved; but then she hid her face in the pillow, and cried more quietly, but more bitterly.

Then some one knocked; she would not answer. Then came a voice, saying, "Katharine." It was Aunt Barbara's, but it was rather wavering. She would not answer, so the door was opened, and the steps, scarcely audible in the rustling of the silk, came in; and Kate felt that her aunt was looking at her, wondered whether she had better put out her head, ask pardon, and have it over, but was afraid; and presently heard the moire antique go sweeping away again.

And then the foolish child heartily wished she had spoken, and was seized with desperate fears of the morrow, more of the shame of hearing of her tears than of any punishment. Why had she not been braver?

After a time came a light, and Josephine moving about quietly, and putting away the clothes that had been left on the floor. Kate was not afraid of her, but her caressing consolations and pity would have only added to the miserable sense of shame; so there was no sign, no symptom of being awake, though it was certain that before Josephine went away, the candle was held so as to cast a light over all that was visible of the face. Kate could not help hearing the low muttering of the Frenchwoman, who was always apt to talk to herself: "Asleep! Ah, yes! She sleeps profoundly. How ugly la petite has made herself! What cries! Ah, she is like Miladi her aunt! a demon of a temper!"

Kate restrained herself till the door was shut again, and then rolled over and over, till she had made a strange entanglement of her bed- clothes, and brought her passion to an end by making a mummy of herself, bound hand and foot, snapping with her month all the time, as if she longed to bite.

"O you horrible Frenchwoman! You are a flatterer, a base flatterer; such as always haunt the great! I hate it all. I a demon of a temper? I like Aunt Barbara? Oh, you wretch! I'll tell Aunt Barbara a to-morrow, and get you sent away!"

Those were some of Kate's fierce angry thoughts in her first vexation; but with all her faults, she was not a child who ever nourished rancour or malice; and though she had been extremely wounded at first, yet she quickly forgave.

By the time she had smoothed out her sheet, and settled matters between it and her blanket, she had begun to think more coolly. "No, no, I won't. It would be horribly dishonourable and all that to tell Aunt Barbara. Josephine was only thinking out loud; and she can't help what she thinks. I was very naughty; no wonder she thought so. Only next time she pets me, I will say to her, 'You cannot deceive me, Josephine; I like the plain truth better than honeyed words.'"

And now that Kate had arrived at the composition of a fine speech that would never be made, it was plain that her mind was pretty well composed. That little bit of forgiveness, though it had not even cost an effort, had been softening, soothing, refreshing; it had brought peacefulness; and Kate lay, not absolutely asleep, but half dreaming, in the summer twilight, in the soft undefined fancies of one tired out with agitation.

She was partly roused by the various sounds in the house, but not startled-- the light nights of summer always diminished her alarms; and she heard the clocks strike, and the bell ring for prayers, the doors open and shut, all mixed in with her hazy fancies. At last came the silken rustlings up the stairs again, and the openings of bed-room doors close to her.

Kate must have gone quite to sleep, for she did not know when the door was opened, and how the soft voices had come in that she heard over her.

"Poor little dear! How she has tossed her bed about! I wonder if we could set the clothes straight without wakening her."

How very sweet and gentle Aunt Jane's voice was in that low cautious whisper.

Some one--and Kate knew the peculiar sound of Mrs. Lacy's crape--was moving the bed-clothes as gently as she could.

"Poor little dear!" again said Lady Jane; "it is very sad to see a child who has cried herself to sleep. I do wish we could manage her better. Do you think the child is happy?" she ended by asking in a wistful voice.

"She has very high spirits," was the answer.

"Ah, yes! her impetuosity; it is her misfortune, poor child! Barbara is so calm and resolute, that--that--" Was Lady Jane really going to regret anything in her sister? She did not say it, however; but Kate heard her sigh, and add, "Ah, well! if I were stronger, perhaps we could make her happier; but I am so nervous. I must try not to look distressed when her spirits do break out, for perhaps it is only natural. And I am so sorry to have brought all this on her, and spoilt those poor children's pleasure!"

Lady Jane bent over the child, and Kate reared herself up on a sudden, threw her arms round her neck, and whispered, "Aunt Jane, dear Aunt Jane, I'll try never to frighten you again! I am so sorry."

"There, there; have I waked you? Don't, my dear; your aunt will hear. Go to sleep again. Yes, do."

But Aunt Jane was kissing and fondling all the time; and the end of this sad naughty evening was, that Kate went to sleep with more softness, love, and repentance in her heart, than there had been since her coming to Bruton Street.

CHAPTER VII.

Lady Caergwent was thoroughly ashamed and bumbled by that unhappy evening. She looked so melancholy and subdued in the morning, with her heavy eyelids and inflamed eyes, and moved so meekly and sadly, without daring to look up, that Lady Barbara quite pitied her, and said--more kindly than she had ever spoken to her before:

"I see you are sorry for the exposure last night, so we will say no more about it. I will try to forget it. I hope our friends may."

That hope sounded very much like "I do not think they will;" and truly Kate felt that it was not in the nature of things that they ever should. She should never have forgotten the sight of a little girl in that frenzy of passion! No, she was sure that their mamma and papa knew all about it, and that she should never be allowed to play with them again, and she could not even wish to meet them, she should be miserably ashamed, and would not know which way to look.

She said not one word about meeting them, and for the first day or two even begged to walk in the square instead of the park; and she was so good and steady with her lessons, and so quiet in her movements, that she scarcely met a word of blame for a whole week.

One morning, while she was at breakfast with Lady Barbara and Mrs. Lacy, the unwonted sound of a carriage stopping, and of a double knock, was heard. In a moment the colour flushed into Lady Barbara's face, and her eyes lighted: then it passed away into a look of sadness. It had seemed to her for a moment as if the bright young nephew who had been the light and hope of her life, were going to look in on her; and it had only brought the remembrance that he was gone for ever, and that in his stead there was only the poor little girl, to whom rank was a misfortune, and who seemed as if she would never wear it becomingly. Kate saw nothing of all this; she was only eager and envious for some change and variety in these long dull days. It was Lord de la Poer and his daughter Adelaide, who the next moment were in the room; and she remembered instantly that she had heard that this was to be Adelaide's birthday, and wished her many happy returns in all due form, her heart beating the while with increasing hope that the visit concerned herself.

And did it not? Her head swam round with delight and suspense, and she could hardly gather up the sense of the words in which Lord de la Poer was telling Lady Barbara that Adelaide's birthday was to be spent at the Crystal Palace at Sydenham; that the other girls were gone to the station with their mother, and that he had come round with Adelaide to carry off Kate, and meet the rest at ten o'clock. Lady de la Poer would have written, but it had only boon settled that morning on finding that he could spare the day.

Kate squeezed Adelaide's hand in an agony. Oh! would that aunt let her go?

"You would like to come?" asked Lord de la Poer, bending his pleasant eyes on her. "Have you ever been there?"

"Never! Oh, thank you! I should like it so much! I never saw any exhibition at all, except once the Gigantic Cabbage!--May I go, Aunt Barbara?"

"Really you are very kind, after--"

"Oh, we never think of AFTERS on birthdays!--Do we, Addie?"

"If you are so very good, perhaps Mrs. Lacy will kindly bring her to meet you."

"I am sure," said he, turning courteously to that lady, "that we should be very sorry to give Mrs. Lacy so much trouble. If this is to be a holiday to everyone, I am sure you would prefer the quiet day."

No one could look at the sad face and widow's cap without feeling that so it must be, even without the embarrassed "Thank you, my Lord, if--"

"If--if Katharine were more to be trusted," began Lady Barbara.

"Now, Barbara," he said in a drolly serious fashion, "if you think the Court of Chancery would seriously object, say so at once."

Lady Barbara could not keep the corners of her mouth quite stiff, but she still said, "You do not know what you are undertaking."

"Do you deliberately tell me that you think myself and Fanny, to say nothing of young Fanny, who is the wisest of us all, unfit to be trusted with this one young lady?" said he, looking her full in the face, and putting on a most comical air: "It is humiliating, I own."

"Ah! if Katharine were like your own daughters, I should have no fears," said the aunt. "But--However, since you are so good--if she will promise to be very careful--"

"Oh yes, yes, Aunt Barbara!"

"I make myself responsible," said Lord de la Poer. "Now, young woman, run off and get the hat; we have no time to lose."

Kate darted off and galloped up the stairs at a furious pace, shouted "Josephine" at the top; and then, receiving no answer, pulled the bell violently; after which she turned round, and obliged Adelaide with a species of dancing hug, rather to the detriment of that young lady's muslin jacket.

"I was afraid to look back before," she breathlessly said, as she released Adelaide; "I felt as if your papa were Orpheus, when

'Stern Proserpine relented, And gave him back the fair--'

and I was sure Aunt Barbara would catch me like Eurydice, if I only looked back."

"What a funny girl you are, to be thinking about Orpheus and Eurydice!" said Adelaide. "Aren't you glad?"

"Glad? Ain't I just! as Charlie would say. Oh dear! your papa is a delicious man; I'd rather have him for mine than anybody, except Uncle Wardour!"

"I'd rather have him than anyone," said the little daughter. "Because he is yours," said Kate; "but somehow, though he is more funny and good-natured than Uncle Wardour, I wouldn't--no, I shouldn't like him so well for a papa. I don't think he would punish so well."

"Punish!" cried Adelaide. "Is that what you want? Why, Mamma says children ought to be always pleasure and no trouble to busy fathers. But there, Kate; you are not getting ready--and we are to be at the station at ten."

"I am waiting for Josephine! Why doesn't she come?" said Kate, ringing violently again.

"Why don't you get ready without her?"

"I don't know where anything is! It is very tiresome of her, when she knows I never dress myself," said Kate fretfully.

"Don't you? Why, Grace and I always dress ourselves, except for the evening.

Let me help you. Are not those your boots?"

Kate rushed to the bottom of the attic stairs, and shouted "Josephine" at the top of her shrill voice; then, receiving no answer, she returned, condescended to put on the boots that Adelaide held up to her, and noisily pulled out some drawers; but not seeing exactly what she wanted, she again betook herself to screams of her maid's name, at the third of which out burst Mrs. Bartley in a regular state of indignation: "Lady Caergwent! Will your Ladyship hold your tongue! There's Lady Jane startled up, and it's a mercy if her nerves recover it the whole day--making such a noise as that!"

"But Josephine won't come, and I'm going out, Bartley," said Kate piteously. "Where is Josephine?"

"Gone out, my Lady, so it is no use making a piece of work," said Bartley crossly, retreating to Lady Jane.

Kate was ready to cry; but behold, that handy little Adelaide had meantime picked out a nice black silk cape, with hat and feather, gloves and handkerchief, which, if not what Kate had intended, were nice enough for anything, and would have--some months ago--seemed to the orphan at the parsonage like robes of state. Kind Adelaide held them up so triumphantly, that Kate could not pout at their being only everyday things; and as she began to put them on, out came Mrs. Bartley again, by Lady Jane's orders, pounced upon Lady Caergwent, and made her repent of all wishes for assistance by beginning upon her hair, and in spite of all wriggles and remonstrances, dressing her in the peculiarly slow and precise manner by which a maid can punish a troublesome child; until finally Kate--far too much irritated for a word of thanks, tore herself out of her hands, caught up her gloves, and flew down-stairs as if her life depended on her speed. She thought the delay much longer than it had really been, for she found Lord de la Poer talking so earnestly to her aunt, that he hardly looked up when she came in--something about her Uncle Giles in India, and his coming home--which seemed to be somehow becoming possible--though at a great loss to himself; but there was no making it out; and in a few minutes he rose, and after some fresh charges from Lady Barbara to her niece "not to forgot herself," Kate was handed into the carriage, and found herself really off.

Then the tingle of wild impatience and suspense subsided, and happiness began! It had not been a good beginning, but it was very charming now.

Adelaide and her father were full of jokes together, so quick and bright that Kate listened instead of talking. She had almost lost the habit of merry chatter, and it did not come to her quickly again; but she was greatly entertained; and thus they came to the station, where Lady de la Poer and her other three girls were awaiting them, and greeted Kate with joyful faces.

They were the more relieved at the arrival of the three, because the station was close and heated, and it was a very warm summer day, so that the air was extremely oppressive.

"It feels like thunder," said some one. And thenceforth Kate's perfect felicity was clouded. She had a great dislike to a thunder- storm, and she instantly began asking her neighbours if they REALLY thought it would be thunder.

"I hope it will," said Lady Fanny; "it would cool the air, and sound so grand in those domes."

Kate thought this savage, and with an imploring look asked Lady de la Poer if she thought there would be a storm.

"I can't see the least sign of one," was the answer. "See how clear the sky is!" as they steamed out of the station.

"But do you think there will be one to-day?" demanded Kate.

"I do not expect it," said Lady de la Poer, smiling; "and there is no use in expecting disagreeables."

"Disagreeables! O Mamma, it would be such fun," cried Grace, "if we only had a chance of getting wet through!"

Here Lord de la Poer adroitly called off the public attention from the perils of the clouds, by declaring that he wanted to make out the fourth line of an advertisement on the banks, of which he said he had made out one line as he was whisked by on each journey he had made; and as it was four times over in four different languages, he required each damsel to undertake one; and there was a great deal of laughing over which it should be that should undertake each language. Fanny and Mary were humble, and sure they could never catch the German; and Kate, more enterprising, undertook the Italian. After all, while they were chattering about it, they went past the valuable document, and were come in sight of the "monsters" in the Gardens; and Lord de la Poer asked Kate if she would like to catch a pretty little frog; to which Mary responded, "Oh, what a tadpole it must have been!" and the discovery that her friends had once kept a preserve of tadpoles to watch them turn into frogs, was so delightful as entirely to dissipate all remaining thoughts of thunder, and leave Kate free for almost breathless amazement at the glittering domes of glass, looking like enormous bubbles in the sun.

What a morning that was, among the bright buds and flowers, the wonders of nature and art all together! It was to be a long day, and no hurrying; so the party went from court to court at their leisure, sat down, and studied all that they cared for, or divided according to their tastes. Fanny and Mary wanted time for the wonderful sculptures on the noble gates in the Italian court; but the younger girls preferred roaming more freely, so Lady de la Poer sat down to take care of them, while her husband undertook to guide the wanderings of the other three.

He particularly devoted himself to Kate, partly in courtesy as to the guest of the party, partly because, as he said, he felt himself responsible for her; and she was in supreme enjoyment, talking freely to one able and willing to answer her remarks and questions, and with the companionship of girls of her own age besides. She was most of all delighted with the Alhambra--the beauty of it was to her like a fairy tale; and she had read Washington Irving's "Siege of Granada," so that she could fancy the courts filled with the knightly Moors, who were so noble that she could not think why they were not Christians--nay, the tears quite came into her eyes as she looked up in Lord de la Poer's face, and asked why nobody converted the Abencerrages instead of fighting with them!

It was a pity that Kate always grew loud when she was earnest; and Lord de la Poer's interest in the conversation was considerably lessened by the discomfort of seeing some strangers looking surprised at the five syllables in the squeaky voice coming out of the mouth of so small a lady.

"Gently, my dear," he softly said; and Kate for a moment felt it hard that the torment about her voice should pursue her even in such moments, and spoil the Alhambra itself.

However, her good humour recovered the next minute, at the Fountain of Lions. She wanted to know how the Moors came to have lions; she thought she had heard that no Mahometans were allowed to represent any living creature, for fear it should be an idol. Lord de la Poer said she was quite right, and that the Mahometans think these forms will come round their makers at the last day, demanding to have souls given to them; but that her friends, the Moors of Spain, were much less strict than any others of their faith. She could see, however, that the carving of such figures was a new art with them, since these lions were very rude and clumsy performances for people who could make such delicate tracery as they had seen within. And then, while Kate was happily looking with Adelaide at the orange trees that completed the Spanish air of the court, and hoping to see the fountain play in the evening, he told Grace that it was worth while taking people to see sights if they had as much intelligence and observation as Kate had, and did not go gazing idly about, thinking of nothing.

He meant it to stir up his rather indolent-minded Grace--he did not mean the countess to hear it; but some people's eyes and ears are wonderfully quick at gathering what is to their own credit, and Kate, who had not heard a bit of commendation for a long time, was greatly elated.

Luckily for appearances, she remembered how Miss Edgeworth's Frank made himself ridiculous by showing off to Mrs. J-- , and how she herself had once been overwhelmed by the laughter of the Wardour family for having rehearsed to poor Mrs. Brown all the characters of the gods of the Northmen--Odin, Thor, and all-- when she had just learnt them. So she was more careful than before not to pour out all the little that she knew; and she was glad she had not committed herself, for she had very nearly volunteered the information that Pompeii was overwhelmed by Mount Etna, before she heard some one say Vesuvius, and perceived her mistake, feeling as if she had been rewarded for her modesty like a good child in a book.

She applauded herself much more for keeping back her knowledge till it was wanted, than for having it; but this self-satisfaction looked out in another loop-hole. She avoided pedantry, but she was too much elated not to let her spirits get the better of her; and when Lady de la Poer and the elder girls came up, they found her in a suppressed state of capering, more like a puppy on its hind logs, than like a countess or any other well-bred child.

The party met under the screen of kings and queens, and there had some dinner, at one of the marble tables that just held them pleasantly. The cold chicken and tongue were wonderfully good on that hot hungry day, and still better were the strawberries that succeeded them; and oh! what mirth went on all the time! Kate was chattering fastest of all, and loudest--not to say the most nonsensically. It was not nice nonsense--that was the worst of it-- it was pert and saucy. It was rather the family habit to laugh at Mary de la Poer for ways that were thought a little fanciful; and Kate caught this up, and bantered without discretion, in a way not becoming towards anybody, especially one some years her elder. Mary was good-humoured, but evidently did not like being asked if she had stayed in the mediaeval court, because she was afraid the great bulls of Nineveh would run at her with their five legs.

"She will be afraid of being teazed by a little goose another time," said Lord de la Poer, intending to give his little friend a hint that she was making herself very silly; but Kate took it quite another way, and not a pretty one, for she answered, "Dear me, Mary, can't you say bo to a goose!"

"Say what?" cried Adelaide, who was always apt to be a good deal excited by Kate; and who had been going off into fits of laughter at all these foolish sallies.

"It is not a very nice thing to say," answered her mother gravely; "so there is no occasion to learn it."

Kate did take the hint this time, and coloured up to the ears, partly with vexation, partly with shame. She sat silent and confused for several minutes, till her friends took pity on her, and a few good- natured words about her choice of an ice quite restored her liveliness. It is well to be good-humoured; but it is unlucky, nay, wrong, when a check from friends without authority to scold, does not suffice to bring soberness instead of rattling giddiness. Lady de la Poer was absolutely glad to break up the dinner, so as to work off the folly and excitement by moving about, before it should make the little girl expose herself, or infect Adelaide.

They intended to have gone into the gardens till four o'clock, when the fountains were to play; but as they moved towards the great door, they perceived a dark heavy cloud was hiding the sun that had hitherto shone so dazzlingly through the crystal walls.

"That is nice," said Lady Fanny; "it will be cool and pleasant now before the rain."

"If the rain is not imminent," began her father.

"Oh! is it going to be a thunder-storm?" cried Kate. "Oh dear! I do so hate thunder! What shall I do?" cried she; all her excitement turning into terror.

Before anyone could answer her, there was a flash of bright white light before all their eyes, and a little scream.

"She's struck! she's struck!" cried Adelaide, her hands before her eyes.

For Kate had disappeared. No, she was in the great pond, beside which they had been standing, and Mary was kneeling on the edge, holding fast by her frock. But before the deep voice of the thunder was roaring and reverberating through the vaults, Lord de la Poer had her in his grasp, and the growl had not ceased before she was on her feet again, drenched and trembling, beginning to be the centre of a crowd, who were running together to help or to see the child who had been either struck by lightning or drowned.

"Is she struck? Will she be blind?" sobbed Adelaide, still with her hands before her eyes; and the inquiry was echoed by the nearer people, while more distant ones told each other that the young lady was blind for life.

"Struck! nonsense!" said Lord de la Poer; "the lightning was twenty miles off at least. Are you hurt, my dear?"

"No," said Kate, shaking herself, and answering "No," more decidedly. "Only I am so wet, and my things stick to me."

"How did it happen?" asked Grace.

"I don't know. I wanted to get away from the thunder!" said bewildered Kate.

Meantime, an elderly lady, who had come up among the spectators, was telling Lady de la Poer that she lived close by, and insisting that the little girl should be taken at once to her house, put to bed, and her clothes dried. Lady de la Poer was thankful to accept the kind offer without loss of time; and in the fewest possible words it was settled that she would go and attend to the little drowned rat, while her girls should remain with their father at the palace till the time of going home, when they would meet at the station. They must walk to the good lady's house, be the storm what it would, as the best chance of preventing Kate from catching cold. She looked a rueful spectacle, dripping so as to make a little pool on the stone floor; her hat and feather limp and streaming; her hair in long lank rats' tails, each discharging its own waterfall; her clothes, ribbons, and all, pasted down upon her! There was no time to be lost; and the stranger took her by one hand, Lady de la Poer by the other, and exchanging some civil speeches with one another half out of breath, they almost swung her from one step of the grand stone stairs to another, and hurried her along as fast as these beplastered garments would let her move. There was no rain as yet, but there was another clap of thunder much louder than the first; but they held Kate too fast to let her stop, or otherwise make herself more foolish.

In a very few minutes they were at the good lady's door; in another minute in her bedroom, where, while she and her maid bustled off to warm the bed, Lady de la Poer tried to get the clothes off--a service of difficulty, when every tie held fast, every button was slippery, and the tighter garments fitted like skins. Kate was subdued and frightened; she gave no trouble, but all the help she gave was to pull a string so as to make a hopeless knot of the bow that her friend had nearly undone.

However, by the time the bed was warm the dress was off, and the child, rolled up in a great loose night-dress of the kind lady's, was installed in it, feeling--sultry day though it were--that the warm dryness was extremely comfortable to her chilled limbs. The good lady brought her some hot tea, and moved away to the window, talking in a low murmuring voice to Lady de la Poer. Presently a fresh flash of lightning made her bury her head in the pillow; and there she began thinking how hard it was that the thunder should come to spoil her one day's pleasure; but soon stopped this, remembering Who sends storm and thunder, and feeling afraid to murmur. Then she remembered that perhaps she deserved to be disappointed. She had been wild and troublesome, had spoilt Adelaide's birthday, teazed Mary, and made kind Lady de la Poer grave and displeased.

She would say how sorry she was, and ask pardon. But the two ladies still stood talking. She must wait till this stranger was gone. And while she was waiting--how it was she knew not--but Countess Kate was fast asleep.

CHAPTER VIII.

When Kate opened her eyes again, and turned her face up from the pillow, she saw the drops on the window shining in the sun, and Lady de la Poer, with her bonnet off, reading under it.

All that had happened began to return on Kate's brain in a funny medley; and the first thing she exclaimed was, "Oh! those poor little fishes, how I must have frightened them!"

"My dear!"

"Do you think I did much mischief?" said Kate, raising herself on her arm. "I am sure the fishes must have been frightened, and the water- lilies broken. Oh! you can't think how nasty their great coiling stems were--just like snakes! But those pretty blue and pink flowers! Did it hurt them much, do you think--or the fish?"

"I should think the fish had recovered the shock," said Lady de la Poer, smiling; "but as to the lilies, I should be glad to be sure you had done yourself as little harm as you have to them."

"Oh no," said Kate, "I'm not hurt--if Aunt Barbara won't be terribly angry. Now I wouldn't mind that, only that I've spoilt Addie's birthday, and all your day. Please, I'm very sorry!"

She said this so sadly and earnestly, that Lady de la Poer came and gave her a kind hiss of forgiveness, and said:

"Never mind, the girls are very happy with their father, and the rest is good for me."

Kate thought this very comfortable and kind, and clung to the kind hand gratefully; but though it was a fine occasion for one of the speeches she could have composed in private, all that came out of her mouth was, "How horrid it is--the way everything turns out with me!"

"Nay, things need not turn out horrid, if a certain little girl would keep herself from being silly."

"But I AM a silly little girl!" cried Kate with emphasis. "Uncle Wardour says he never saw such a silly one, and so does Aunt Barbara!"

"Well, my dear," said Lady de la Poer very calmly, "when clever people take to being silly, they can be sillier than anyone else."

"Clever people!" cried Kate half breathlessly.

"Yes," said the lady, "you are a clever child; and if you made the most of yourself, you could be very sensible, and hinder yourself from being foolish and unguarded, and getting into scrapes."

Kate gasped. It was not pleasant to be in a scrape; and yet her whole self recoiled from being guarded and watchful, even though for the first time she heard she was not absolutely foolish. She began to argue, "I was naughty, I know, to teaze Mary; and Mary at home would not have let me; but I could not help the tumbling into the pond. I wanted to get out of the way of the lightning."

"Now, Kate, you ARE trying to show how silly you can make yourself."

"But I can't bear thunder and lightning. It frightens me so, I don't know what to do; and Aunt Jane is just as bad. She always has the shutters shut."

"Your Aunt Jane has had her nerves weakened by bad health; but you are young and strong, and you ought to fight with fanciful terrors."

"But it is not fancy about lightning. It does kill people."

"A storm is very awful, and is one of the great instances of God's power. He does sometimes allow His lightnings to fall; but I do not think it can be quite the thought of this that terrifies you, Kate, for the recollection of His Hand is comforting."

"No," said Kate honestly, "it is not thinking of that. It is that the glare--coming no one knows when--and the great rattling clap are so--so frightful!"

"Then, my dear, I think all you can do is to pray not only for protection from lightning and tempest, but that you may be guarded from the fright that makes you forget to watch yourself, and so renders the danger greater! You could not well have been drowned where you fell; but if it had been a river--"

"I know," said Kate.

"And try to get self-command. That is the great thing, after all, that would hinder things from being horrid!" said Lady de la Poer, with a pleasant smile, just as a knock came to the door, and the maid announced that it was five o'clock, and Miss's things were quite ready; and in return she was thanked, and desired to bring them up.

"Miss!" said Kate, rather hurt: "don't they know who we are?"

"It is not such a creditable adventure that we should wish to make your name known," said Lady de la Poer, rather drily; and Kate blushed, and became ashamed of herself.

She was really five minutes before she recovered the use of her tongue, and that was a long time for her. Lady de la Poer meantime was helping her to dress, as readily as Josephine herself could have done, and brushing out the hair, which was still damp. Kate presently asked where the old lady was.

"She had to go back as soon as the rain was over, to look after a nephew and niece, who are spending the day with her. She said she would look for our party, and tell them how we were getting on."

"Then I have spoilt three people's pleasure more!" said Kate ruefully. "Is the niece a little girl?"

"I don't know; I fancy her grown up, or they would have offered clothes to you."

"Then I don't care!" said Kate.

"What for?"

"Why, for not telling my name. Once it would have been like a fairy tale to Sylvia and me, and have made up for anything, to see a countess--especially a little girl. But don't you think seeing me would quite spoil that?"

Lady de la Poer was so much amused, that she could not answer at first; and Kate began to feel as if she had been talking foolishly, and turned her back to wash her hands.

"Certainly, I don't think we are quite as well worth seeing as the Crystal Palace! You put me in mind of what Madame Campan said. She had been governess to the first Napoleon's sisters; and when, in the days of their grandeur, she visited them, one of them asked her if she was not awe-struck to find herself among so much royalty. 'Really,' she said, 'I can't be much afraid of queens whom I have whipped!'"

"They were only mock queens," said Kate.

"Very true. But, little woman, it is ALL mockery, unless it is the SELF that makes the impression; and I am afraid being perched upon any kind of pedestal makes little faults and follies do more harm to others. But come, put on your hat: we must not keep Papa waiting."

The hat was the worst part of the affair; the colour of the blue edge of the ribbon had run into the white, and the pretty soft feather had been so daggled in the wet, that an old hen on a wet day was respectability itself compared with it, and there was nothing for it but to take it out; and even then the hat reminded Kate of a certain Amelia Matilda Bunny, whose dirty finery was a torment and a by-word in St. James's Parsonage. Her frock and white jacket had been so nicely ironed out, as to show no traces of the adventure; and she disliked all the more to disfigure herself with such a thing on her head for the present, as well as to encounter Aunt Barbara by-and-by.

"There's no help for it," said Lady de la Poer, seeing her disconsolately surveying it; "perhaps it will not be bad for you to feel a few consequences from your heedlessness."

Whether it were the hat or the shock, Kate was uncommonly meek and subdued as she followed Lady de la Poer out of the room; and after giving the little maid half a sovereign and many thanks for having so nicely repaired the damage, they walked back to the palace, and up the great stone stairs, Kate hanging down her head, thinking that everyone was wondering how Amelia Matilda Bunny came to be holding by the hand of a lady in a beautiful black lace bonnet and shawl, so quiet and simple, and yet such a lady!

She hardly even looked up when the glad exclamations of the four girls and their father sounded around her, and she could not bear their inquiries whether she felt well again. She knew that she owed thanks to Mary and her father, and apologies to them all; but she had not manner enough to utter them, and only made a queer scrape with her foot, like a hen scratching out corn, hung her head, and answered "Yes."

They saw she was very much ashamed, and they were in a hurry besides; so when Lord de la Poer had said he had given all manner of thanks to the good old lady, he took hold of Kate's hand, as if he hardly ventured to let go of her again, and they all made the best of their way to the station, and were soon in full career along the line, Kate's heart sinking as she thought of Aunt Barbara. Fanny tried kindly to talk to her; but she was too anxious to listen, made a short answer, and kept her eyes fixed on the two heads of the party, who were in close consultation, rendered private by the noise of the train.

"If ever I answer for anyone again!" said Lord de la Poer. "And now for facing Barbara!"

"You had better let me do that."

"What! do you think I am afraid?" and Kate thought the smile on his lip very cruel, as she could not hear his words.

"I don't do you much injustice in thinking so," as he shrugged up his shoulders like a boy going to be punished; "but I think Barbara considers you as an accomplice in mischief, and will have more mercy if I speak."

"Very well! I'm not the man to prevent you. Tell Barbara I'll undergo whatever she pleases, for having ever let go the young lady's hand! She may have me up to the Lord Chancellor if she pleases!"

A little relaxation in the noise made these words audible; and Kate, who knew the Lord Chancellor had some power over her, and had formed her notions of him from a picture, in a history book at home, of Judge Jefferies holding the Bloody Assize, began to get very much frightened; and her friends saw her eyes growing round with alarm, and not knowing the exact cause, pitied her; Lord de la Poer seated her upon his knee, and told her that Mamma would take her home, and take care Aunt Barbara did not punish her.

"I don't think she will punish me," said Kate; "she does not often! But pray come home with me!" she added, getting hold of the lady's hand.

"What would she do to you, then?"

"She would--only--be dreadful!" said Kate.

Lord de la Poer laughed; but observed, "Well, is it not enough to make one dreadful to have little girls taking unexpected baths in public? Now, Kate, please to inform me, in confidence, what was the occasion of that remarkable somerset."

"Only the lightning," muttered Kate.

"Oh! I was not certain whether your intention might not have been to make that polite address to an aquatic bird, for which you pronounced Mary not to have sufficient courage!"

Lady de la Poer, thinking this a hard trial of the poor child's temper, was just going to ask him not to tease her; but Kate was really candid and good tempered, and she said, "I was wrong to say that! It was Mary that had presence of mind, and I had not."

"Then the fruit of the adventure is to be, I hope, Look Before you Leap!--Eh, Lady Caergwent?"

And at the same time the train stopped, and among kisses and farewells, Kate and kind Lady de la Poer left the carriage, and entering the brougham that was waiting for them, drove to Bruton Street; Kate very grave and silent all the way, and shrinking behind her friend in hopes that the servant who opened the door would not observe her plight--indeed, she took her hat off on the stairs, and laid it on the table in the landing.

To her surprise, the beginning of what Lady de la Poer said was chiefly apology for not having taken better care of her. It was all quite true: there was no false excuse made for her, she felt, when Aunt Barbara looked ashamed and annoyed, and said how concerned she was that her niece should be so unmanageable; and her protector answered,

"Not that, I assure you! She was a very nice little companion, and we quite enjoyed her readiness and intelligent interest; but she was a little too much excited to remember what she was about when she was startled."

"And no wonder," said Lady Jane. "It was a most tremendous storm, and I feel quite shaken by it still. You can't be angry with her for being terrified by it, Barbara dear, or I shall know what you think of me;--half drowned too--poor child!"

And Aunt Jane put her soft arm round Kate, and put her cheek to hers. Perhaps the night of Kate's tears had really made Jane resolved to try to soften even Barbara's displeasure; and the little girl felt it very kind, though her love of truth made her cry out roughly, "Not half drowned! Mary held me fast, and Lord de la Poer pulled me out!"

"I am sure you ought to be extremely thankful to them," said Lady Barbara, "and overcome with shame at all the trouble and annoyance you have given!"

Lady de la Poer quite understood what the little girl meant by her aunt being dreadful. She would gladly have protected her; but it was not what could be begged off like punishment, nor would truth allow her to say there had been no trouble nor annoyance. So what she did say was, "When one has ten children, one reckons upon such things!" and smiled as if they were quite pleasant changes to her.

"Not, I am sure, with your particularly quiet little girls," said Aunt Barbara. "I am always hoping that Katharine may take example by them."

"Take care what you hope, Barbara," said Lady de la Poer, smiling: "and at any rate forgive this poor little maiden for our disaster, or my husband will be in despair."

"I have nothing to forgive," said Lady Barbara gravely. "Katharine cannot have seriously expected punishment for what is not a moral fault. The only difference will be the natural consequences to herself of her folly.--You had better go down to the schoolroom, Katharine, have your tea, and then go to bed; it is nearly the usual time."

Lady de la Poer warmly kissed the child, and then remained a little while with the aunts, trying to remove what she saw was the impression, that Kate had been complaining of severe treatment, and taking the opportunity of telling them what she herself thought of the little girl. But though Aunt Barbara listened politely, she could not think that Lady de la Poer knew anything about the perverseness, heedlessness, ill-temper, disobedience, and rude ungainly ways, that were so tormenting. She said no word about them herself, because she would not expose her niece's faults; but when her friend talked Kate's bright candid conscientious character, her readiness, sense, and intelligence, she said to herself, and perhaps justly, that here was all the difference between at home and abroad, an authority and a stranger.

Meantime, Kate wondered what would be the natural consequences of her folly. Would she have a rheumatic fever or consumption, like a child in a book?--and she tried breathing deep, and getting up a little cough, to see if it was coming! Or would the Lord Chancellor hear of it? He was new bugbear recently set up, and more haunting than even a gunpowder treason in the cellars! What did he do with the seals? Did he seal up mischievous heiresses in closets, as she had seen a door fastened by two seals and a bit of string? Perhaps the Court of Chancery was full of such prisons! And was the woolsack to smother them with, like the princes in the Tower?

It must be owned that it was only when half asleep at night that Kate was so absurd. By day she knew very well that the Lord Chancellor was only a great lawyer; but she also knew that whenever there was any puzzle or difficulty about her or her affairs, she always heard something mysteriously said about applying to the Lord Chancellor, till she began to really suspect that it was by his commands that Aunt Barbara was so stern with her; and that if he knew of her fall into the pond, something terrible would come of it. Perhaps that was why the De la Poers kept her name so secret!

She trembled as she thought of it; and here was another added to her many terrors. Poor little girl! If she had rightly feared and loved One, she would have had no room for the many alarms that kept her heart fluttering!

CHAPTER IX.

It may be doubted whether Countess Kate ever did in her childhood discover what her Aunt Barbara meant by the natural consequences of her folly, but she suffered from them nevertheless. When the summer was getting past its height of beauty, and the streets were all sun and misty heat, and the grass in the parks looked brown, and the rooms were so close that even Aunt Jane had one window open, Kate grew giddy in the head almost every morning, and so weary and dull all day that she had hardly spirit to do anything but read story- books. And Mrs. Lacy was quite poorly too, though not saying much about it; was never quite without a head-ache, and was several times obliged to send Kate out for her evening walk with Josephine.

It was high time to be going out of town; and Mrs. Lacy was to go and be with her son in his vacation.

This was the time when Kate and the Wardours had hoped to be together. But "the natural consequence" of the nonsense Kate had talked, about being "always allowed" to do rude and careless things, and her wild rhodomontade about romping games with the boys, had persuaded her aunts that they were very improper people for her to be with, and that it would be wrong to consent to her going to Oldburgh.

That was one natural consequence of her folly. Another was that when the De la Poers begged that she might spend the holidays with them, and from father and mother downwards were full of kind schemes for her happiness and good, Lady Barbara said to her sister that it was quite impossible; these good friends did not know what they were asking, and that the child would again expose herself in some way that would never be forgotten, unless she were kept in their own sight till she had been properly tamed and reduced to order.

It was self-denying in Lady Barbara to refuse that invitation, for she and her sister would have been infinitely more comfortable together without their trouble-some countess--above all when they had no governess to relieve them of her. The going out of town was sad enough to them, for they had always paid a long visit at Caergwent Castle, which had felt like their home through the lifetime of their brother and nephew; but now it was shut up, and their grief for their young neph-ew came back all the more freshly at the time of year when they were used to be kindly entertained by him in their native home.

But as they could not go there, they went to Bournemouth and the first run Kate took upon the sands took away all the giddiness from her head, and put an end to the tired feeling in her limbs! It really was a run! Aunt Barbara gave her leave to go out with Josephine; and though Josephine said it was very sombre and savage, between the pine-woods and the sea, Kate had not felt her heart leap with such fulness of enjoyment since she had made snow-balls last winter at home. She ran down to the waves, and watched them sweep in and curl over and break, as if she could never have enough of them; and she gazed at the grey outline of the Isle of Wight opposite, feeling as if there was something very great in really seeing an island.

When she came in, there was so much glow on her brown check, and her eyelids looked so much less heavy, that both the aunts gazed at her with pleasure, smiled to one another, and Lady Jane kissed her, while Lady Barbara said, "This was the right thing."

She was to be out as much as possible, so her aunt made a set of new rules for the day. There was to be a walk before breakfast; then breakfast; then Lady Barbara heard her read her chapter in the Bible, and go through her music. And really the music was not half as bad as might have been expected with Aunt Barbara. Kate was too much afraid of her to give the half attention she had paid to poor Mrs. Lacy--fright and her aunt's decision of manner forced her to mind what she was about; and though Aunt Barbara found her really very dull and unmusical, she did get on better than before, and learnt something, though more like a machine than a musician.

Then she went out again till the hottest part of the day, during which a bit of French and of English reading was expected from her, and half an hour of needle-work; then her dinner; and then out again- -with her aunts this time, Aunt Jane in a wheeled-chair, and Aunt Barbara walking with her--this was rather dreary; but when they went in she was allowed to stay out with Josephine, with only one interval in the house for tea, till it grew dark, and she was so sleepy with the salt wind, that she was ready for bed, and had no time to think of the Lord Chancellor.

At first, watching those wonderful and beautiful waves was pleasure enough; and then she was allowed, to her wonder and delight, to have a holland dress, and dig in the sand, making castles and moats, or rocks and shipwrecks, with beautiful stories about them; and sometimes she hunted for the few shells and sea-weeds there, or she sat down and read some of her favourite books, especially poetry--it suited the sea so well; and she was trying to make Ellen's Isle and all the places of the "Lady of the Lake" in sand, only she never had time to finish them, and they always were either thrown down or washed away before she could return to them.

But among all these amusements, she was watching the families of children who played together, happy creatures! The little sturdy boys, that dabbled about so merrily, and minded so little the "Now Masters" of their indignant nurses; the little girls in brown hats, with their baskets full; the big boys, that even took off shoes, and dabbled in the shallow water; the great sieges of large castles, where whole parties attacked and defended--it was a sort of melancholy glimpse of fairy-land to her, for she had only been allowed to walk on the beach with Josephine on condition she never spoke to the other children.

Would the Lord Chancellor be after her if she did? Her heart quite yearned for those games, or even to be able to talk to one of those little damsels; and one day when a bright-faced girl ran after her with a piece of weed that she had dropped, she could hardly say "thank you" for her longing to say more; and many were the harangues she composed within herself to warn the others not to wish to change places with her, for to be a countess was very poor fun indeed.

However, one morning at the end of the first week, Kate looked up from a letter from Sylvia, and said with great glee, "Aunt Barbara! O Aunt Barbara! Alice and the other Sylvia--Sylvia Joanna--are coming! I may play with them, mayn't I?"

"Who are they?" said her aunt gravely.

"Uncle Wardour's nieces," said Kate; "Sylvia's cousins, you know, only we never saw them; but they are just my age; and it will be such fun--only Alice is ill, I believe. Pray--please--let me play with them!" and Kate had tears in her eyes.

"I shall see about it when they come."

"Oh, but--but I can't have them there--Sylvia's own, own cousins--and not play with them! Please, Aunt Barbara!"

"You ought to know that this impetuosity never disposes me favourably, Katharine; I will inquire and consider."

Kate had learnt wisdom enough not to say any more just then; but the thought of sociability, the notion of chattering freely to young companions, and of a real game at play, and the terror of having all this withheld, and of being thought too proud and haughty for the Wardours, put her into such an agony, that she did not know what she was about, made mistakes even in reading, and blundered her music more than she had over done under Lady Barbara's teaching; and then, when her aunt reproved her, she could not help laying down her head and bursting into a fit of crying. However, she had not forgotten the terrible tea-drinking, and was resolved not to be as bad as at that time, and she tried to stop herself, exclaiming between her sobs, "O Aunt Bar--bar--a,--I--can--not--help it!" And Lady Barbara did not scold or look stern. Perhaps she saw that the little girl was really trying to chock herself, for she said quite kindly, "Don't, my dear."

And just then, to Kate's great wonder, in came Lady Jane, though it was full half an hour earlier than she usually left her room; and Lady Barbara looked up to her, and said, quite as if excusing herself, "Indeed, Jane, I have not been angry with her."

And Kate, somehow, understanding that she might, flung herself down by Aunt Jane, and hid her face in her lap, not crying any more, though the sobs were not over, and feeling the fondling hands on her hair very tender and comforting, though she wondered to hear them talk as if she were asleep or deaf--or perhaps they thought their voices too low, or their words too long and fine for her to understand; nor perhaps did she, though she gathered their drift well enough, and that kind Aunt Jane was quite pleading for herself in having come to the rescue.

"I could not help it, indeed--you remember Lady de la Poer, Dr. Woodman, both--excitable, nervous temperament--almost hysterical."

"This unfortunate intelligence--untoward coincidence--" said Lady Barbara. "But I have been trying to make her feel I am not in anger, and I hope there really was a struggle for self-control."

Kate took her head up again at this, a little encouraged; and Lady Jane kissed her forehead, and repeated, "Aunt Barbara was not angry with you, my dear."

"No, for I think you have tried to conquer yourself," said Lady Barbara. She did not think it wise to tell Kate that she thought she could not help it, though oddly enough, the very thing had just been said over the child's head, and Kate ventured on it to get up, and say quietly, "Yes, it was not Aunt Barbara's speaking to me that made me cry, but I am so unhappy about Alice and Sylvia Joanna;" and a soft caress from Aunt Jane made her venture to go on. "It is not only the playing with them, though I do wish for that very very much indeed; but it would be so unkind, and so proud and ungrateful, to despise my own cousin's cousins!"

This was more like the speeches Kate made in her own head than anything she had ever said to her aunts; and it was quite just besides, and not spoken in naughtiness, and Lady Barbara did not think it wrong to show that she attended to it. "You are right, Katharine," she said; "no one wishes you to be either proud or ungrateful. I would not wish entirely to prevent you from seeing the children of the family, but it must not be till there is some acquaintance between myself and their mother, and I cannot tell whether you can be intimate with them till I know what sort of children they are. Much, too, must depend on yourself, and whether you will behave well with them."

Kate gave a long sigh, and looked up relieved; and for some time she and her aunt were not nearly so much at war as hitherto, but seemed to be coming to a somewhat better understanding.

Yet it rather puzzled Kate. She seemed to herself to have got this favour for crying for it; and it was a belief at home, not only that nothing was got by crying, but that if by some strange chance it were, it never came to good; and she began the more to fear some disappointment about the expected Wardours.

For two or three days she was scanning every group on the sands with all her might, in hopes of some likeness to Sylvia, but at last she was taken by surprise: just as she was dressed, and Aunt Barbara was waiting in the drawing-room for Aunt Jane, there came a knock at the door, and "Mrs. Wardour" was announced.

In came a small, quiet-looking lady in mourning, and with her a girl of about Kate's own age; there was some curtseying and greeting between the two ladies, and her aunt said, "Here is my niece.--Come and speak to Mrs. Wardour, my dear," and motioned her forwards.

Now to be motioned forwards by Aunt Barbara always made Kate shrink back into herself, and the presence of a little girl before elders likewise rendered her shy and bashful, so she came forth as if intensely disgusted, put out her hand as if she were going to poke, and muttered her favourite "--do" so awkwardly and coldly, that Lady Barbara felt how proud and ungracious it looked, and to make up said, "My niece has been very eager for your coming." And then the two little girls drew off into the window, and looked at each other under their eyelashes in silence.

Sylvia Joanna Wardour was not like her namesake at home, Sylvia Katharine. She was a thin, slight, quiet-looking child, with so little to note about her face, that Kate was soon wondering at her dress being so much smarter than her own was at present. She herself had on a holland suit with a deep cape, which, except that they were adorned with labyrinths of white braid, were much what she had worn at home, also a round brown hat, shading her face from the sun; whereas Sylvia's face was exposed by a little turban hat so deeply edged with blue velvet, that the white straw was hardly seen; had a little watered-silk jacket, and a little flounced frock of a dark silk figured with blue, that looked slightly fuzzed out; and perhaps she was not at ease in this fine dress, for she stood with her head down, and one hand on the window-sill, pretending to look out of window, but really looking at Kate.

Meanwhile the two grown-up ladies were almost as stiff and shy, though they could not keep dead silence like the children. Mrs. Wardour had heard before that Lady Barbara Umfraville was a formidable person, and was very much afraid of her; and Lady Barbara was not a person to set anyone at ease.

So there was a little said about taking the liberty of calling, for her brother-in-law was so anxious to hear of Lady Caergwent: and Lady Barbara said her niece was very well and healthy, and had only needed change of air.

And then came something in return about Mrs. Wardour's other little girl, a sad invalid, she said, on whose account they were come to Bournemouth; and there was a little more said of bathing, and walking, and whether the place was full; and then Mrs. Wardour jumped up and said she was detaining Lady Barbara, and took leave; Kate, though she had not spoken a word to Sylvia Wardour, looking at her wistfully with all her eyes, and feeling more than usually silly.

And when the guests were gone her aunt told her how foolish her want of manner was, and how she had taken the very means to make them think she was not glad to see them. She hung down her head, and pinched the ends of her gloves; she knew it very well, but that did not make it a bit more possible to find a word to say to a stranger before the elders, unless the beginning were made for her as by the De la Poers.

However, she knew it would be very different out of doors, and her heart bounded when her aunt added, "They seem to be quiet, lady-like, inoffensive people, and I have no objection to your associating with the little girl in your walks, as long as I do not see that it makes you thoughtless and ungovernable."

"Oh, thank you, thank you, Aunt Barbara!" cried Kate, with a bouncing bound that did not promise much for her thought or her governableness; but perhaps Lady Barbara recollected what her own childhood would have been without Jane, for she was not much discomposed, only she said,

"It is very odd you should be so uncivil to the child in her presence, and so ecstatic now! However, take care you do not get too familiar. Remember, these Wardours are no relations, and I will not have you letting them call you by your Christian name."

Kate's bright looks sank. That old married-woman sound, Lady Caergwent, seemed as if it would be a bar between her and the free childish fun she hoped for. Yet when so much had been granted, she must not call her aunt cross and unkind, though she did think it hard and proud.

Perhaps she was partly right; but after all, little people cannot judge what is right in matters of familiarity. They have only to do as they are told, and they may be sure of this, that friendship and respect depend much more on what people are in themselves than on what they call one another.

This lady was the widow of Mr. Wardour's brother, and lived among a great clan of his family in a distant county, where Mary and her father had sometimes made visits, but the younger ones never. Kate was not likely to have been asked there, for it was thought very hard that she should be left on the hands of her aunt's husband: and much had been said of the duty of making her grand relations provide for her, or of putting her into the "Clergy Orphan Asylum." And there had been much displeasure when Mr. Wardour answered that he did not think it right that a child who had friends should live on the charity intended for those who had none able to help them; and soon after the decision he had placed his son Armyn in Mr. Brown's office, instead of sending him to the University. All the Wardours were much vexed then; but they were not much better pleased when the little orphan had come to her preferment, and he made no attempt to keep her in his hands, and obtain the large sum allowed for her board--only saying that his motherless household was no place for her, and that he could not at once do his duty by her and by his parish. They could not understand the real love and uprightness that made him prefer her advantage to his own--what was right to what was convenient.

Mrs. George Wardour had not scolded her brother-in-law for his want of prudence and care for his own children's interests; but she had agreed with those who did; and this, perhaps, made her feel all the more awkward and shy when she was told that she MUST go and call upon the Lady Umfravilles, whom the whole family regarded as first so neglectful and then so ungrateful, and make acquaintance with the little girl who had once been held so cheap. She was a kind, gentle person, and a careful, anxious mother, but not wishing to make great acquaintance, nor used to fine people, large or small, and above all, wrapped up in her poor little delicate Alice.

The next time Kate saw her she was walking by the side of Alice's wheeled-chair, and Sylvia by her side, in a more plain and suitable dress. Kate set off running to greet them; but at a few paces from them was seized by a shy fit, and stood looking and feeling like a goose, drawing great C's with the point of her parasol in the sand; Josephine looking on, and thinking how "bete" English children were. Mrs. Wardour was not much less shy; but she knew she must make a beginning, and so spoke in the middle of Kate's second C: and there was a shaking of hands, and walking together.

They did not get on very well: nobody talked but Mrs. Wardour, and she asked little frightened questions about the Oldburgh party, as she called them, which Kate answered as shortly and shyly--the more so from the uncomfortable recollection that her aunt had told her that this was the very way to seem proud and unkind; but what could she do? She felt as if she were frozen up stiff, and could neither move nor look up like herself. At last Mrs. Wardour said that Alice would be tired, and must go in; and then Kate managed to blurt out a request that Sylvia might stay with her. Poor Sylvia looked a good deal scared, and as if she longed to follow her mamma and sister; but the door was shut upon her, and she was left alone with those two strange people--the Countess and the Frenchwoman!

However, Kate recovered the use of her limbs and tongue in a moment, and instantly took her prisoner's hand, and ran off with her to the corner where the scenery of Loch Katrine had so often been begun, and began with great animation to explain. This--a hole that looked as if an old hen had been grubbing in it--was Loch Katrine.

"Loch Katharine--that's yours! And which is to be Loch Sylvia?" said the child, recovering, as she began to feel by touch, motion, and voice, that she had only to do with a little girl after all.

"Loch nonsense!" said Kate, rather bluntly. "Did you never hear of the Lochs, the Lakes, in Scotland?"

"Loch Lomond, Loch Katrine, Loch Awe, Loch Ness?--But I don't do my geography out of doors!"

"'Tisn't geography; 'tis the 'The Lady of the Lake.'"

"Is that a new game?"

"Dear me! did you never read 'The Lady of the Lake?'--Sir Walter Scott's poem -

'The summer dawn's reflected hue--'"

"Oh! I've learnt that in my extracts; but I never did my poetry task out of doors!"

"'Tisn't a task--'tis beautiful poetry! Don't you like poetry better than anything?"

"I like it better than all my other lessons, when it is not very long and hard."

Kate felt that her last speech would have brought Armyn and Charlie down on her for affectation, and that it was not strictly true that she liked poetry better than anything, for a game at romps, and a very amusing story, were still better things; so she did not exclaim at the other Sylvia's misunderstanding, but only said, "'The Lady of the Lake' is story and poetry too, and we will play at it."

"And how?"

"I'll tell you as we go on. I'm the King--that is, the Knight of Snowdon--James Fitzjames, for I'm in disguise, you know; and you're Ellen."

"Must I be Ellen? We had a horrid nurse once, who used to slap us, and was called Ellen."

"But it was her name. She was Ellen Douglas, and was in banishment on an island with her father. You are Ellen, and Josephine is your old harper--Allan Bane; she talks French, you know, and that will do for Highland: Gallic and Gaelic sound alike, you know. There! Then I'm going out hunting, and my dear gallant grey will drop down dead with fatigue, and I shall lose my way; and when you hear me wind my horn too-too, you get upon your hoop--that will be your boat, you know--and answer 'Father!' and when I too-too again, answer 'Malcolm!' and then put up your hand behind your ear, and stand listening

"With locks thrown back and lips apart, Like monument of Grecian art;"
and then I'll tell you what to do."

Away scudded the delighted Kate; and after having lamented her gallant grey, and admired the Trosachs, came up too-tooing through her hand with all her might, but found poor Ellen, very unlike a monument of Grecian art, absolutely crying, and Allan Bane using his best English and kindest tones to console her.

"Miladi l'a stupefaite--la pauvre petite!" began Josephine; and Kate in consternation asking what was the matter, and Josephine encouraging her, it was all sobbed out. She did not like to be called Ellen--and she thought it unkind to send her into banishment-- and she had fancied she was to get astride on her hoop, which she justly thought highly improper--and above all, she could not bear to say 'Father'--because -

"I never thought you would mind that," said Kate, rather abashed. "I never did; and I never saw my papa or mamma either."

"No--so you didn't care."

"Well then," said Kate gravely, "we won't play at that. Let's have 'Marmion' instead; and I'll be killed."

"But I don't like you to be killed."

"It is only in play."

"Please--please, let us have a nice play!"

"Well, what do you call a nice play?"

"Alice and I used to drive hoops."

"That's tiresome! My hoop always tumbles down: think of something else."

"Alice and I used to play at ball; but there's no ball here!"

"Then I'll stuff my pocket-handkerchief with seaweed, and make one;" and Kate spread out her delicate cambric one--not quite so fit for such a purpose as the little cheap cotton ones at home, that Mary tried in vain to save from cruel misuse.

"Here's a famous piece! Look, it is all wriggled; it is a mermaid's old stay-lace that she has used and thrown away. Perhaps she broke it in a passion because her grandmother made her wear so many oyster- shells on her tail!"

"There are no such creatures as mermaids," said Sylvia, looking at her solemnly.

This was not a promising beginning; Sylvia Joanna was not a bit like Sylvia Katharine, nor like Adelaide and Grace de la Poer; yet by seeing each other every day, she and Kate began to shake together, and become friends.

There was no fear of her exciting Kate to run wild; she was a little pussy-cat in her dread of wet, and guarded her clothes as if they could feel--indeed, her happiest moments were spent in the public walks by Alice's chair, studying how the people were dressed; but still she thought it a fine thing to be the only child in Bournemouth who might play with the little Countess, and was so silly as to think the others envied her when she was dragged and ordered about, bewildered by Kate's loud rapid talk about all kinds of odd things in books, and distressed at being called on to tear through the pine- woods, or grub in wet sand. But it was not all silly vanity: she was a gentle, loving little girl, very good-natured, and sure to get fond of all who were kind to her; and she liked Kate's bright ways and amusing manner-- perhaps really liking her more than if she had understood her better; and Kate liked her, and rushed after her on every occasion, as the one creature with whom it was possible to play and to chatter.

No, not quite the one; for poor sick Alice was better for talk and quiet play than her sister. She read a great deal; and there was an exchange of story-books, and much conversation over them, between her and Kate--indeed, the spirit and animation of this new friend quite made her light up, and brighten out of her languor whenever the shrill laughing voice came near. And Kate, after having got over her first awe at coming near a child so unlike herself, grew very fond of her, and felt how good and sweet and patient she was. She never ran off to play till Alice was taken in-doors; and spent all her spare time in-doors in drawing picture stories, which were daily explained to the two sisters at some seat in the pine-woods.

There was one very grand one, that lasted all the latter part of the stay at Bournemouth--as the evenings grew longer, and Kate had more time for preparing it, at the rate of four or five scenes a day, drawn and painted--being the career of a very good little girl, whose parents were killed in a railway accident, (a most fearful picture was that--all blunders being filled up by spots of vermilion blood and orange-coloured flame!) and then came all the wonderful exertions by which she maintained her brothers and sisters, taught them, and kept them in order.

They all had names; and there was a naughty little Alexander, whose monkey tricks made even Sylvia laugh. Sylvia was very anxious that the admirable heroine, Hilda, should be rewarded by turning into a countess; and could not enter into Kate's first objection--founded on fact--that it could not be without killing all the brothers. "Why couldn't it be done in play, like so many other things?" To which Kate answered, "There is a sort of true in play;" but as Sylvia could not understand her, nor she herself get at her own idea, she went on to her other objection, a still more startling one--that "She couldn't wish Hilda anything so nasty!"

And this very ignoble word was long a puzzle to Alice and Sylvia.

Thus the time at the sea-side was very happy--quite the happiest since Kate's change of fortune. The one flaw in those times on the sands was when she was alone with Sylvia and Josephine; not in Sylvia's dulness--that she had ceased to care about--but in a little want of plain dealing. Sylvia was never wild or rude, but she was not strictly obedient when out of sight; and when Kate was shocked would call it very unkind, and caress and beseech her not to tell.

They were such tiny things, that they would hardly bear mention; but one will do as a specimen. Sylvia was one of those very caressing children who can never be happy without clinging to their friends, kissing them constantly, and always calling them dear, love, and darling.

Now, Mrs. Wardour knew it was not becoming to see all this embracing in public, and was sure besides that Lady Barbara would not like to see the Countess hung upon in Sylvia's favourite way; so she forbade all such demonstrations except the parting and meeting kiss. It was a terrible grievance to Sylvia--it seemed as if her heart could not love without her touch; but instead of training herself in a little self-control and obedience, she thought it "cross;" and Mamma was no sooner out of sight than her arm was around Kate's waist. Kate struggled at first--it did not suit her honourable conscientiousness; but then Sylvia would begin to cry at the unkindness, say Kate did not love her, that she would not be proud if she was a countess: and Kate gave in, liked the love--of which, poor child! she got so little--and let Sylvia do as she pleased, but never without a sense of disobedience and dread of being caught.

So, too, about her title. Sylvia called her darling, duck, and love, and she called Sylvia by plenty of such names; but she had been obliged to tell of her aunt's desire--that Katharine and Kate should never be used.

Sylvia's ready tears fell; but the next day she came back cheerful, with the great discovery that darling Lady Caergwent might be called K, her initial, and the first syllable of her title. It was the cleverest invention Sylvia had ever made; and she was vexed when Kate demurred, honestly thinking that her aunts would like it worse than even Kate, and that therefore she ought not to consent.

But when Sylvia coaxingly uttered, "My own dear duck of a K," and the soft warm arm squeezed her, and the eyes would have been weeping, and the tongue reproaching in another moment, she allowed it to go on--it was so precious and sweet to be loved; and she told Sylvia she was a star in the dark night.

No one ever found out those, and one or two other, instances of small disobedience. They were not mischievous, Josephine willingly overlooked them, and there was nothing to bring them to light. It would have been better for Sylvia if her faults had been of a sort that brought attention on them more easily!

Meanwhile, Lady Barbara had almost found in her a model child--except for her foolish shy silence before her elders, before whom she always whispered--and freely let the girls be constantly together. The aunt little knew that this meek well-behaved maiden was giving the first warp to that upright truth that had been the one sterling point of Kate's character!

CHAPTER X.

It had been intended that Mrs. Lacy should rejoin her pupil at Bournemouth at the end of six weeks; but in her stead came a letter saying that she was unwell, and begging for a fortnight's grace. At the fortnight's end came another letter; to which Lady Barbara answered that all was going on so well, that there was no need to think of returning till they should all meet in London on the 1st of October.

But before that 1st, poor Mrs. Lacy wrote again, with great regret and many excuses for the inconvenience she was causing. Her son and her doctor had insisted on her resigning her situation at once; and they would not even allow her to go back until her place could be supplied.

"Poor thing!" said Lady Jane. "I always thought it was too much for her. I wish we could have made her more comfortable: it would have been such a thing for her!"

"So it would," answered Lady Barbara, "if she had had to do with any other child. A little consideration or discretion, such as might have been expected from a girl of eleven years old towards a person in her circumstances, would have made her happy, and enabled her to assist her son. But I have given up expecting feeling from Katharine."

That speech made Kate swell with anger at her aunt's tone and in her anger she forgot to repent of having been really thoughtless and almost unkind, or to recollect how differently her own gentle Sylvia at home would have behaved to the poor lady. She liked the notion of novelty, and hoped for a new governess as kind and bright as Miss Oswald.

Moreover, she was delighted to find that Mrs. George Wardour was going to live in London for the present, that Alice might be under doctors, and Sylvia under masters. Kate cared little for the why, but was excessively delighted with plans for meeting, hopes of walks, talks, and tea-drinkings together; promises that the other dear Sylvia should come to meet her; and above all, an invitation to spend Sylvia Joanna's birthday with her on the 21st of October, and go all together either to the Zoological Gardens or to the British Museum, according to the weather.

With these hopes, Kate was only moderately sorry to leave the sea and pine-trees behind her, and find herself once more steaming back to London, carrying in her hand a fine blue and white travelling-bag, worked for her by her two little friends, but at which Lady Barbara had coughed rather dryly. In the bag were a great many small white shells done up in twists of paper, that pretty story "The Blue Ribbons," and a small blank book, in which, whenever the train stopped, Kate wrote with all her might. For Kate had a desire to convince Sylvia Joanna that one was much happier without being a countess, and she thought this could be done very touchingly and poetically by a fable in verse; so she thought she had a very good idea by changing the old daisy that pined for transplantation and found it very unpleasant, into a harebell.

A harebell blue on a tuft of moss In the wind her bells did toss.

That was her beginning; and the poor harebell was to get into a hot- house, where they wanted to turn her into a tall stately campanula, and she went through a great deal from the gardeners. There was to be a pretty fairy picture to every verse; and it would make a charming birthday present, much nicer than anything that could be bought; and Kate kept on smiling to herself as the drawings came before her mind's eye, and the rhymes to her mind's ear.

So they came home; but it was odd, the old temper of the former months seemed to lay hold of Kate as soon as she set foot in the house in Bruton Street, as if the cross feelings were lurking in the old corners.

She began by missing Mrs. Lacy very much. The kind soft governess had made herself more loved than the wayward child knew; and when Kate had run into the schoolroom and found nobody sitting by the fire, no sad sweet smile to greet her, no one to hear her adventures, and remembered that she had worried the poor widow, and that she would never come back again, she could have cried, and really had a great mind to write to her, ask her pardon, and say she was sorry. It would perhaps have been the beginning of better things if she had; but of all things in the world,

what prevented her? Just this--that she had an idea that her aunt expected it of her!
O Kate! Kate!

So she went back to the harebell, and presently began rummaging among her
books for a picture of one to copy; and just then Lady Barbara came in, found half a
dozen strewn on the floor, and ordered her to put them tidy, and then be dressed.
That put her out, and after her old bouncing fashion she flew upstairs, caught her
frock in the old hitch at the turn, and half tore off a flounce.

No wonder Lady Barbara was displeased; and that was the beginning of things
going wrong--nay, worse than before the going to Bournemouth. Lady Barbara was
seeking for a governess, but such a lady as she wished for was not to be found in a
day; and in the meantime she was resolved to do her duty by her niece, and watched
over her behaviour, and gave her all the lessons that she did not have from masters.

Whether it was that Lady Barbara did not know exactly what was to be expected of a little girl, or whether Kate was more fond of praise than was good for
her, those daily lessons were more trying than ever they had been. Generally she
had liked them; but with Aunt Barbara, the being told to sit upright, hold her book
straight, or pronounce her words rightly, always teased her, and put her out of humour at the beginning. Or she was reminded of some failure of yesterday, and it
always seemed to her unjust that bygones should not be bygones; or even when she
knew she had been doing her best, her aunt always thought she could have done
better, so that she had no heart or spirit to try another time, but went on in a dull,
save-trouble way, hardly caring to exert herself to avoid a scolding, it was so certain
to come.

It was not right--a really diligent girl would have won for herself the peaceful
sense of having done her best, and her aunt would have owned it in time; whereas
poor Kate's resistance only made herself and her aunt worse to each other every
day, and destroyed her sense of duty and obedience more and more.

Lady Barbara could not be always with her, and when once out of sight there
was a change. If she were doing a lesson with one of her masters, she fell into a
careless attitude in an instant, and would often chatter so that there was no calling
her to order, except by showing great determination to tell her aunt. It made her
feel both sly and guilty to behave so differently out of sight, and yet now that she
had once begun she seemed unable to help going on and she was sure, foolish child,

that Aunt Barbara's strictness made her naughty!

Then there were her walks. She was sent out with Josephine in the morning and desired to walk nowhere but in the Square; and in the afternoon she and Josephine were usually set down by the carriage together in one of the parks, and appointed where to meet it again after Lady Jane had taken her airing when she was well enough, for she soon became more ailing than usual. They were to keep in the quiet paths, and not speak to anyone.

But neither Josephine nor her young lady had any turn for what was "triste." One morning, when Kate was in great want of a bit of India-rubber, and had been sighing because of the displeasure she should meet for having lost her own through using it in play-hours, Josephine offered to take her--only a little out of her way--to buy a new piece.

Kate knew this was not plain dealing, and hated herself for it, but she was tired of being scolded, and consented! And then how miserable she was; how afraid of being asked where she had been; how terrified lest her aunt should observe that it was a new, not an old, piece; how humiliated by knowing she was acting untruth!

And then Josephine took more liberties. When Kate was walking along the path, thinking how to rhyme to "pride," she saw Josephine talking over the iron rail to a man with a beard; and she told her maid afterwards that it was wrong; but Josephine said, "Miladi had too good a heart to betray her," and the man came again and again, and once even walked home part of the way with Josephine, a little behind the young lady.

Kate was desperately affronted, and had a great mind to complain to her aunts. But then Josephine could have told that they had not been in the Square garden at all that morning, but in much more entertaining streets! Poor Kate, these daily disobediences did not weigh on her nearly as much as the first one did; it was all one general sense of naughtiness!

Working at her harebell was the pleasantest thing she did, but her eagerness about it often made her neglectful and brought her into scrapes. She had filled one blank book with her verses and pictures, some rather good, some very bad; and for want of help and correction she was greatly delighted with her own performance, and thought it quite worthy of a little ornamental album, where she could write out the verses and gum in the drawings.

"Please, Aunt Barbara, let me go to the Soho Bazaar to-day?"

"I cannot take you there, I have an engagement."

"But may I not go with Josephine?"

"Certainly not. I would not trust you there with her. Besides, you spend too much upon trumpery, as it is."

"I don't want it for myself; I want something to get ready for Sylvia's birthday--the Sylvia that is come to London, I mean."

"I do not approve of a habit of making presents."

"Oh! but, Aunt Barbara, I am to drink tea with her on her birthday, and spend the day, and go to the Zoological Gardens, and I have all ready but my presents! and it will not be in time if you won't let me go to-day."

"I never grant anything to pertinacity," answered Lady Barbara. "I have told you that I cannot go with you to-day, and you ought to submit."

"But the birthday, Aunt Barbara!"

"I have answered you once, Katharine; you ought to know better than to persist."

Kate pouted, and the tears swelled in her eyes at the cruelty of depriving her of the pleasure of making her purchase, and at having her beautiful fanciful production thus ruined by her aunt's unkindness. As she sat over her geography lesson, out of sight of her own bad writing, her broken-backed illuminated capitals, her lumpy campanulas, crooked-winged fairies, queer perspective, and dabs of blue paint, she saw her performance not as it was, but as it was meant to be, heard her own lines without their awkward rhymes and bits like prose, and thought of the wonder and admiration of all the Wardour family, and of the charms of having it secretly lent about as a dear simple sweet effusion of the talented young countess, who longed for rural retirement. And down came a great tear into the red trimming of British North America, and Kate unadvisedly trying to wipe it up with her handkerchief, made a red smear all across to Cape Verd! Formerly she would have exclaimed at once; now she only held up the other side of the book that her aunt might not see, and felt very shabby all the time. But Lady Barbara was reading over a letter, and did not look. If Kate had not been wrapt up in herself, she would have seen that anxious distressed face.

There came a knock to the schoolroom door. It was Mr. Mercer, the doctor, who always came to see Lady Jane twice a week, and startled and alarmed, Lady Barbara sprang up. "Do you want me, Mr. Mercer? I'll come."

"No, thank you," said the doctor, coming in. "It was only that I promised I would look at this little lady, just to satisfy Lady Jane, who does not think her quite well."

Kate's love of being important always made her ready to be looked at by Mr. Mercer, who was a kind, fatherly old gentleman, not greatly apt to give physic, very good-natured, and from his long attendance more intimate with the two sisters than perhaps any other person was. Lady Barbara gave an odd sort of smile, and said, "Oh! very well!" and the old gentleman laughed as the two bright clear eyes met his, and said, "No great weight there, I think! Only a geography fever, eh? Any more giddy heads lately, eh? Or only when you make cheeses?"

"I can't make cheeses now, my frocks are so short," said Kate, whose spirits always recovered with the least change.

"No more dreams?"

"Not since I went to Bournemouth."

"Your tongue." And as Kate, who had a certain queer pleasure in the operation, put out the long pinky member with its ruddier tip, quivering like an animal, he laughed again, and said, "Thank you, Lady Caergwent; it is a satisfaction once in a way to see something perfectly healthy! You would not particularly wish for a spoonful of cod-liver oil, would you?"

Kate laughed, made a face, and shook her head.

"Well," said the doctor as he released her, "I may set Lady Jane's mind at rest. Nothing the matter there with the health."

"Nothing the matter but perverseness, I am afraid," said Lady Barbara, as Kate stole back to her place, and shut her face in with the board of her atlas. "It is my sister who is the victim, and I cannot have it go on. She is so dreadfully distressed whenever the child is in disgrace that it is doing her serious injury. Do you not see it, Mr. Mercer?"

"She is very fond of the child," said Mr. Mercer.

"That is the very thing! She is constantly worrying herself about her, takes all her naughtiness for illness, and then cannot bear to see her reproved. I assure you I am forced for my sister's sake to overlook many things which I know I ought not to pass by." (Kate shuddered.) "But the very anxiety about her is doing great harm."

"I thought Lady Jane nervous and excited this morning," said Mr. Mercer: "but that seemed to me to be chiefly about the Colonel's return."

"Yes," said Lady Barbara, "of course in some ways it will be a great pleasure; but it is very unlucky, after staying till the war was over, that he has had to sell out without getting his promotion. It will make a great difference!"

"On account of his son's health, is it not?"

"Yes; of course everything must give way to that, but it is most unfortunate. The boy has never recovered from his wound at Lucknow, and they could not bear to part, or they ought to have sent him home with his mother long ago; and now my brother has remained at his post till he thought he could be spared; but he has not got his promotion, which he must have had in a few months."

"When do you expect him?"

"They were to set off in a fortnight from the time he wrote, but it all depended on how Giles might be. I wish we knew; I wish there could be any certainty, this is so bad for my sister. And just at this very time, without a governess, when some children would be especially thoughtful and considerate, that we should have this strange fit of idleness and perverseness! It is very trying; I feel quite hopeless sometimes!"

Some children, as Lady Barbara said, would have been rendered thoughtful and considerate by hearing such a conversation as this, and have tried to make themselves as little troublesome to their elders as possible; but there are others who, unless they are directly addressed, only take in, in a strange dreamy way, that which belongs to the grown-up world, though quick enough to catch what concerns themselves. Thus Kate, though aware that Aunt Barbara thought her naughtiness made Aunt Jane ill, and that there was a fresh threat of the Lord Chancellor upon the return of her great- uncle from India, did not in the least perceive that her Aunt Barbara was greatly perplexed and harassed, divided between her care for her sister and for her niece, grieved for her brother's anxiety, and disappointed that he had been obliged to leave the army, instead of being made a General. The upshot of all that she carried away with her was, that it was very cross of Aunt Barbara to think she made Aunt Jane ill, and very very hard that she could not go to the bazaar.

Lady Jane did not go out that afternoon, and Lady Barbara set her niece and

Josephine down in the Park, saying that she was going into Belgravia, and desiring them to meet her near Apsley House. They began to walk, and Kate began to lament. "If she could only have gone to the bazaar for her album! It was very hard!"

"Eh," Josephine said, "why should they not go? There was plenty of time. Miladi Barbe had given them till four. She would take la petite."

Kate hung back. She knew it was wrong. She should never dare produce the book if she had it.

But Josephine did not attend to the faltered English words, or disposed of them with a "Bah! Miladi will guess nothing!" and she had turned decidedly out of the Park, and was making a sign to a cab. Kate was greatly frightened, but was more afraid of checking Josephine in the open street, and making her dismiss the cab, than of getting into it. Besides, there was a very strong desire in her for the red and gold square book that had imprinted itself on her imagination. She could not but be glad to do something in spite of Aunt Barbara. So they were shut in, and went off along Piccadilly, Kate's feelings in a strange whirl of fright and triumph, amid the clattering of the glasses. Just suppose she saw anyone she knew!

But they got to Soho Square at last; and through the glass door, in among the stalls--that fairy land in general to Kate; but now she was too much frightened and bewildered to do more than hurry along the passages, staring so wildly for her albums, that Josephine touched her, and said, "Tenez, Miladi, they will think you farouche. Ah! see the beautiful wreaths!"

"Come on, Josephine," said Kate impatiently.

But it was not so easy to get the French maid on. A bazaar was felicity to her, and she had her little lady in her power; she stood and gazed, admired, and criticised, at every stall that afforded ornamental wearing apparel or work patterns; and Kate, making little excursions, and coming back again to her side, could not get her on three yards in a quarter of an hour, and was too shy and afraid of being lost, to wander away and transact her own business. At last they did come to a counter with ornamental stationery; and after looking at four or five books, Kate bought a purple embossed one, not at all what she had had in her mind's eye, just because she was in too great a fright to look further; and then step by step, very nearly crying at last, so as to alarm Josephine lest she should really cry, she got her out at last. It was a quarter to four, and Josephine was in vain sure that Miladi Barbe would never be at the place in time; Kate's heart was sick with fright at the thought of the shame of detection.

She begged to get out at the Marble Arch, and not risk driving along Park Lane; but Josephine was triumphant in her certainty that there was time; and on they went, Kate fancying every bay nose that passed the window would turn out to have the brougham, the man-servant, and Aunt Barbara behind it.

At length they were set down at what the Frenchwoman thought a safe distance, and paying the cabman, set out along the side path, Josephine admonishing her lady that it was best not to walk so swiftly, or to look guilty, or they would be "trahies."

But just then Kate really saw the carriage drawn up where there was an opening in the railings, and the servant holding open the door for them. Had they been seen? There was no knowing! Lady Barbara did not say one single word; but that need not have been surprising--only how very straight her back was, how fixed her marble mouth and chin! It was more like Diana's head than ever--Diana when she was shooting all Niobe's daughters, thought Kate, in her dreamy, vague alarm. Then she looked at Josephine on the back seat, to see what she thought of it; but the brown sallow face in the little bonnet was quite still and like itself--beyond Kate's power to read.

The stillness, doubt, and suspense, were almost unbearable. She longed to speak, but had no courage, and could almost have screamed with desire to have it over, end as it would. Yet at last, when the carriage did turn into Bruton Street, fright and shame had so entirely the upper hand, that she read the numbers on every door, wishing the carriage would only stand still at each, or go slower, that she might put off the moment of knowing whether she was found out.

They stopped; the few seconds of ringing, of opening the doors, of getting out, were over. She knew how it would be, when, instead of going upstairs, her aunt opened the schoolroom door, beckoned her in, and said gravely, "Lady Caergwent, while you are under my charge, it is my duty to make you obey me. Tell me where you have been."

There was something in the sternness of that low lady-like voice, and of that dark deep eye, that terrified Kate more than the brightest flash of lightning: and it was well for her that the habit of truth was too much fixed for falsehood or shuffling even to occur to her. She did not dare to do more than utter in a faint voice, scarcely audible "To the bazaar."

"In direct defiance of my commands?"

But the sound of her own confession, the relief of having told, gave Kate spirit to speak; "I know it was naughty," she said, looking up; "I ought not. Aunt Barbara, I have been very naughty. I've been often where you didn't know."

"Tell me the whole truth, Katharine;" and Lady Barbara's look relaxed, and the infinite relief of putting an end to a miserable concealment was felt by the little girl; so she told of the shops she had been at, and of her walks in frequented streets, adding that indeed she would not have gone, but that Josephine took her. "I did like it," she added candidly; "but I know I ought not."

"Yes, Katharine," said Lady Barbara, almost as sternly as ever; "I had thought that with all your faults you were to be trusted."

"I have told you the truth!" cried Kate.

"Now you may have; but you have been deceiving me all this time; you, who ought to set an example of upright and honourable conduct."

"No, no, Aunt!" exclaimed Kate, her eyes flashing. "I never spoke one untrue word to you; and I have not now--nor ever. I never deceived."

"I do not say that you have TOLD untruths. It is deceiving to betray the confidence placed in you."

Kate knew it was; yet she had never so felt that her aunt trusted her as to have the sense of being on honour; and she felt terribly wounded and grieved, but not so touched as to make her cry or ask pardon. She knew she had been audaciously disobedient; but it was hard to be accused of betraying trust when she had never felt that it was placed in her; and yet the conviction of deceit took from her the last ground she had of peace with herself.

Drooping and angry, she stood without a word; and her aunt presently said, "I do not punish you. The consequences of your actions are punishment enough in themselves, and I hope they may warn you, or I cannot tell what is to become of you in your future life, and of all that will depend on you. You must soon be under more strict and watchful care than mine, and I hope the effect may be good. Meantime, I desire that your Aunt Jane may be spared hearing of this affair, little as you seem to care for her peace of mind."

And away went Lady Barbara; while Kate, flinging herself upon the sofa, sobbed out, "I do care for Aunt Jane! I love Aunt Jane! I love her ten hundred times more than you! you horrid cross old Diana! But I have deceived! Oh, I am getting to be a wicked little girl! I never did such things at home. Nobody made me naughty there. But it's the fashionable world. It is corrupting my simplicity. It always does. And I shall be lost! O Mary, Mary! O Papa, Papa! Oh, come and take me home!" And for a little while Kate gasped out these calls, as if she had really thought they would break the spell, and bring her back to Oldburgh.

She ceased crying at last, and slowly crept upstairs, glad to meet no one, and that not even Josephine was there to see her red eyes. Her muslin frock was on the bed, and she managed to dress herself, and run down again unseen; she stood over the fire, so that the housemaid, who brought in her tea, should not see her face; and by the time she had to go to the drawing-room, the mottling of her face had abated under the influence of a story-book, which always drove troubles away for the time.

It was a very quiet evening. Aunt Barbara read bits out of the newspaper, and there was a little talk over them: and Kate read on in her book, to hinder herself from feeling uncomfortable. Now and then Aunt Jane said a few soft words about "Giles and Emily;" but her sister always led away from the subject, afraid of her exciting herself, and getting anxious.

And if Kate had been observing, she would have heard in the weary sound of Aunt Barbara's voice, and seen in those heavy eyelids, that the troubles of the day had brought on a severe headache, and that there was at least one person suffering more than even the young ill- used countess.

And when bed-time came, she learnt more of the "consequences of her actions." Stiff Mrs. Bartley stood there with her candle.

"Where is Josephine?"

"She is gone away, my Lady."

Kate asked no more, but shivered and trembled all over. She recollected that in telling the truth she had justified herself, and at Josephine's expense. She knew Josephine would call it a blackness--a treason. What would become of the poor bright merry Frenchwoman? Should she never see her again? And all because she had not had the firmness to be obedient! Oh, loss of trust! loss of confidence! disobedience! How wicked this place made her! and would there be any end to it?

And all night she was haunted through her dreams with the Lord Chancellor, in his wig, trying to catch her, and stuff her into the woolsack, and Uncle Wardour's voice always just out of reach. If she could only get to him!

CHAPTER XI.

The young countess was not easily broken down. If she was ever so miserable for one hour, she was ready to be amused the next; and though when left to herself she felt very desolate in the present, and much afraid of the future, the least enlivenment brightened her up again into more than her usual spirits. Even an entertaining bit in the history that she was reading would give her so much amusement that she would forget her disgrace in making remarks and asking questions, till Lady Barbara gravely bade her not waste time, and decided that she had no feeling.

It was not more easy to find a maid than a governess to Lady Barbara's mind, nor did she exert herself much in the matter, for, as Kate heard her tell Mr. Mercer, she had decided that the present arrangement could not last; and then something was asked about the Colonel and Mrs. Umfraville; to which the answer was, "Oh no, quite impossible; she could never be in a house with an invalid;" and then ensued something about the Chancellor and an establishment, which, as usual, terrified Kate's imagination.

Indeed that night terrors were at their height, for Mrs. Bartley never allowed dawdling, and with a severely respectful silence made the undressing as brief an affair as possible, brushing her hair till her head tingled all over, putting away the clothes with the utmost speed, and carrying off the candle as soon as she had uttered her grim "Good-night, my Lady," leaving Kate to choose between her pet terrors--either of the Lord Chancellor, or of the house on fire--or a very fine new one, that someone would make away with her to make way for her Uncle Giles and his son to come to her title. Somehow Lady Barbara had contrived to make her exceedingly in awe of her Uncle Giles, the strict stern soldier who was always implicitly obeyed, and who would be so shocked at her. She wished she could hide somewhere when he was coming! But there was one real good bright pleasure near, that would come before her misfortunes; and that was the birthday to be spent at the Wardours'. As to the present, Josephine had had the album in her pocket, and had never restored it, and Kate had begun to feel a distaste to the whole performance, to recollect its faults, and to be ashamed of the entire affair; but that was no reason she should not be very happy with her friends, who had promised to take her to the Zoological Gardens.

She had not seen them since her return to London; they were at Westbourne Road, too far off for her to walk thither even if she had had anyone to go with her, and though they had called, no one had seen them; but she had had two or three notes, and had sent some "story pictures" by the post. And the thoughts of that day of freedom and enjoyment of talking to Alice, being petted by Mrs. Wardour and caressed by Sylvia, seemed to bear her through all the dull morning walks, in which she was not only attended by Bartley, but by the man-servant; all the lessons with her aunt, and the still more dreary exercise which Lady Barbara took with her in some of the parks in the afternoon. She counted the days to the 21st whenever she woke in the morning; and at last Saturday was come, and it would be Monday.

"Katharine," said Lady Barbara at breakfast, "you had better finish your drawing to-day; here is a note from Madame to say it will suit her best to come on Monday instead of Tuesday."

"Oh! but, Aunt Barbara, I am going to Westbourne Road on Monday."

"Indeed! I was not aware of it."

"Oh, it is Sylvia's birthday! and I am going to the Zoological Gardens with them."

"And pray how came you to make this engagement without consulting me?"

"It was all settled at Bournemouth. I thought you knew! Did not Mrs. Wardour ask your leave for me?"

"Mrs. Wardour said something about hoping to see you in London, but I made no decided answer. I should not have allowed the intimacy there if I had expected that the family would be living in London; and there is no reason that it should continue. Constant intercourse would not be at all desirable."

"But may I not go on Monday?" said Kate, her eyes opening wide with consternation.

"No, certainly not. You have not deserved that I should trust you; I do not know whom you might meet there: and I cannot have you going about with any chance person."

"O Aunt Barbara! Aunt Barbara! I have promised!"

"Your promise can be of no effect without my consent."

"But they will expect me. They will be so disappointed!"

"I cannot help that. They ought to have applied to me for my consent."

"Perhaps," said Kate hopefully, "Mrs. Wardour will write to-day. If she does, will you let me go?"

"No, Katharine. While you are under my charge, I am accountable for you, and I will not send you into society I know nothing about. Let me hear no more of this, but write a note excusing yourself, and we will let the coachman take it to the post."

Kate was thoroughly enraged, and forgot even her fears. "I sha'n't excuse myself," she said; "I shall say you will not let me go."

"You will write a proper and gentlewoman-like note," said Lady Barbara quietly, "so as not to give needless offence."

"I shall say," exclaimed Kate more loudly, "that I can't go because you won't let me go near old friends."

"Go into the schoolroom, and write a proper note, Katharine; I shall come presently, and see what you have said," repeated Lady Barbara, commanding her own temper with some difficulty.

Kate flung away into the schoolroom, muttering, and in a tumult of exceeding disappointment, anger, and despair, too furious even to cry, and dashing about the room, calling Aunt Barbara after every horrible heroine she could think of, and pitying herself and her friends, till the thought of Sylvia's disappointment stung her beyond all bearing. She was still rushing hither and thither, inflaming her passion, when her aunt opened the door.

"Where is the note?" she said quietly.

"I have not done it."

"Sit down then this instant, and write," said Lady Barbara, with her Diana face and cool way, the most terrible of all.

Kate sulkily obeyed, but as she seated herself, muttered, "I shall say you won't let me go near them."

"Write as I tell you.--My dear Mrs. Wardour--"

"There."

"I fear you may be expecting to see me on Monday--"

"I don't fear; I know she is."

"Write--I fear you may be expecting me on Monday, as something passed on the subject at Bournemouth; and in order to prevent inconvenience, I write to say that it will not be in my power to call on that day, as my aunt had made a previous engagement for me."

"I am sure I sha'n't say that!" cried Kate, breaking out of all bounds in her indignation.

"Recollect yourself, Lady Caergwent," said Lady Barbara calmly.

"It is not true!" cried Kate passionately, jumping up from her seat. "You had not made an engagement for me! I won't write it! I won't write lies, and you sha'n't make me."

"I do not allow such words or such a manner in speaking to me," said Lady Barbara, not in the least above her usual low voice; and her calmness made Kate the more furious, and jump and dance round with passion, repeating, "I'll never write lies, nor tell lies, for you or anyone; you may kill me, but I won't!"

"That is enough exposure of yourself, Lady Caergwent," said her aunt. "When you have come to your senses, and choose to apologize for insulting me, and show me the letter written as I desire, you may come to me."

And away walked Lady Barbara, as cool and unmoved apparently as if she had been made of cast iron; though within she was as sorry, and hardly less angry, than the poor frantic child she left.

Kate did not fly about now. She was very indignant, but she was proud of herself too; she had spoken as if she had been in a book, and she believed herself persecuted for adhering to old friends, and refusing to adopt fashionable falsehoods, such as she had read of. She was a heroine in her own eyes, and that made her inclined to magnify all the persecution and cruelty. They wanted to shut her up from the friends of her childhood, to force her to be false and fashionable; they had made her naughtier and naughtier ever since she came there; they were teaching her to tell falsehoods now, and to give up the Wardours. She would never never do it! Helpless girl as she was, she would be as brave as the knights and earls her ancestors, and stand up for the truth. But what would they do at her! Oh! could she bear Aunt Barbara's dreadful set Diana face again, and not write as she was told!

The poor weak little heart shrank with terror as she only looked at Aunt Barbara's chair--not much like the Sir Giles de Umfraville she had thought of just now. "And I'm naughty now; I did betray my trust: I'm much naughtier than I was. Oh, if Papa was but here!" And then a light darted into Kate's eye, and a smile came on her lip. "Why should not I go home? Papa would have me again; I know he would! He would die rather than leave his child Kate to be made wicked, and forced to tell lies! Perhaps he'll hide me! Oh, if I could go to school with the children at home in disguise, and let Uncle Giles be Earl of Caergwent if he likes! I've had enough of grandeur! I'll come as Cardinal Wolsey did, when he said he was come to lay his bones among them--and Sylvia and Mary, and Charlie and Armyn--oh, I must go where someone will be kind to me again! Can I really, though? Why not?" and her heart beat violently. "Yes, yes; nothing would happen to me; I know how to manage! If I can only get there, they will hide me from Aunt Barbara and the Lord Chancellor; and even if I had to go back, I should have had one kiss of them all. Perhaps if I don't go now I shall never see them again!"

With thoughts something like these, Kate, moving dreamily, as if she were not sure that it was herself or not, opened her little writing- case, took out her purse, and counted the money. There was a sovereign and some silver; more than enough, as she well knew. Then she took out of a chiffoniere her worked travelling bag, and threw in a few favourite books; then stood and gasped, and opened the door to peep out. The coachman was waiting at the bottom of the stairs for orders, so she drew in her head, looked at her watch, and considered whether her room would be clear of the housemaids. If she could once get safely out of the house she would not be missed till her dinner time, and perhaps then might be supposed sullen, and left alone. She was in a state of great fright, starting violently at every sound; but the scheme having once occurred to her, it seemed as if St. James's Parsonage was pulling her harder and harder every minute; she wondered if there were really such things as heart-strings; if there were, hers must be fastened very tight round Sylvia.

At last she ventured out, and flew up to her own room more swiftly than ever she had darted before! She moved about quietly, and perceived by the sounds in the next room that Mrs. Bartley was dressing Aunt Jane, and Aunt Barbara reading a letter to her. This was surely a good moment; but she knew she must dress herself neatly, and not look scared, if she did not mean to be suspected and stopped; and she managed to get quietly into her little shaggy coat, her black hat and feather and warm gloves--even her boots were remembered--and then whispering to herself, "It can't be wrong to get away from being made to tell stories! I'm going to Papa!" she softly opened the door, went on tip-toe past Lady's Jane's door; then after the first flight of stairs, rushed like the wind, unseen by anyone, got the street door open, pulled it by its outside handle, and heard it shut!

It was done now! She was on the wide world--in the street! She could not have got in again without knocking, ringing, and making her attempt known; and she was far more terrified at the thought of Lady Barbara's stern face and horror at her proceedings than even at the long journey alone.

Every step was a little bit nearer Sylvia, Mary, and Papa--it made her heart bound in the midst of its frightened throbs--every step was farther away from Aunt Barbara, and she could hardly help setting off in a run. It was a foggy day, when it was not so easy to see far, but she longed to be out of Bruton Street, where she might be known; yet when beyond the quiet familiar houses, the sense of being alone, left to herself, began to get very alarming, and she could hardly control herself to walk like a rational person to the cab-stand in Davies Street.

Nobody remarked her; she was a tall girl for her age, and in her sober dark dress, with her little bag, might be taken for a tradesman's daughter going to school, even if anyone had been out who had time to look at her. Trembling, she saw a cab-man make a sign to her, and stood waiting for him, jumped in as he opened his door, and felt as if she had found a refuge for the time upon the dirty red plush cushions and the straw. "To the Waterloo Station," said she, with as much indifference and self-possession as she could manage. The man touched his hat, and rattled off: he perhaps wondering if this were a young runaway, and if he should get anything by telling where she was gone; she working herself into a terrible fright for fear he should be going to drive round and round London, get her into some horrible den of iniquity, and murder her for the sake of her money, her watch, and her clothes. Did not cabmen always do such things? She had quite decided how she would call a policeman, and either die like an Umfraville or offer a ransom of "untold gold," and had gone through all possible catastrophes long before she found herself really safe at the railway station, and the man letting her out, and looking for his money.

The knowledge that all depended on herself, and that any signs of alarm would bring on inquiry, made her able to speak and act so reasonably, that she felt like one in a dream. With better fortune than she could have hoped for, a train was going to start in a quarter of an hour; and the station clerk was much too busy and too much hurried to remark how scared were her eyes, and how trembling her voice, as she asked at his pigeon-hole for "A first-class ticket to Oldburgh, if you please," offered the sovereign in payment, swept up the change, and crept out to the platform.

A carriage had "Oldburgh" marked on it; she tried to open the door, but could not reach the handle; then fancied a stout porter who came up with his key must be some messenger of the Lord Chancellor come to catch her, and was very much relieved when he only said, "Where for, Miss?" and on her answer, "Oldburgh," opened the door for her, and held her bag while she tripped up the steps. "Any luggage, Miss?" "No, thank you." He shot one inquiring glance after her, but hastened away; and she settled herself in the very farthest corner of the carriage, and lived in an agony for the train to set off before her flight should be detected.

Once off, she did not care; she should be sure of at least seeing Sylvia, and telling her uncle her troubles. She had one great start, when the door was opened, and a gentleman peered in; but it was merely to see if there was room, for she heard him say, "Only a child," and in came a lady and two gentlemen, who at least filled up the window so that nobody could see her, while they talked a great deal to someone on the platform. And then after some bell-ringing, whistling, sailing backwards and forwards, and stopping, they were fairly off--getting away from the roofs of London--seeing the sky clear of smoke and fog--getting nearer home every moment; and Countess Kate relaxed her shy, frightened, drawn-up attitude, gave a long breath, felt that the deed was done, and began to dwell on the delight with which she should be greeted at home, and think how to surprise them all!

There was plenty of time for thinking and planning and dreaming, some few possible things, but a great many more most impossible ones. Perhaps the queerest notion of all was her plan for being disguised like a school-child all day, and always noticed for her distinguished appearance by ladies who came to see the school, or overheard talking French to Sylvia; and then in the midst of her exceeding anxiety not to be detected, she could not help looking at her travelling companions, and wondering if they guessed with what a grand personage they had the honour to be travelling! Only a child, indeed! What would they think if they knew? And the little goose held her pocket- handkerchief in her hand, feeling as if it would be like a story if they happened to wonder at the coronet embroidered in the corner; and when she took out a story-book, she would have liked that the fly- leaf should just carelessly reveal the Caergwent written upon it. She did not know that selfishness had thrown out the branch of self- consequence.

However, nothing came of it; they had a great deal too much to say to each other to notice the little figure in the corner; and she had time to read a good deal, settle a great many fine speeches, get into many a fright lest there should be an accident, and finally grow very impatient, alarmed, and agitated before the last station but one was passed, and she began to know the cut of the hedgerow-trees, and the shape of the hills--to feel as if the cattle and sheep in the fields were old friends, and to feel herself at home.

Oldburgh Station! They were stopping at last, and she was on her feet, pressing to the window between the strangers. One of the gentlemen kindly made signs to the porter to let her out, and asked if she had any baggage, or anyone to meet her. She thanked him by a smile and shake of the head; she could not speak for the beating of her heart; she felt almost as much upon the world as when the door in Bruton Street had shut behind her; and besides, a terrible wild fancy had seized her--suppose, just suppose, they were all gone away, or ill, or someone dead! Perhaps she felt it would serve her right, and that was the reason she was in such terror.

CHAPTER XII.

When Kate had left the train, she was still two miles from St. James's; and it was half-past three o'clock, so that she began to feel that she had run away without her dinner, and that the beatings of her heart made her knees ache, so that she had no strength to walk.

She thought her best measure would be to make her way to a pastry- cook's shop that looked straight down the street to the Grammar School, and where it was rather a habit of the family to meet Charlie when they had gone into the town on business, and wanted to walk out with him. He would be out at four o'clock, and there would not be long to wait. So, feeling shy, and even more guilty and frightened than on her first start, Kate threaded the streets she knew so well, and almost gasping with nervous alarm, popped up the steps into the shop, and began instantly eating a bun, and gazing along the street. She really could not speak till she had swallowed a few mouthfuls; and then she looked up to the woman, and took courage to ask if the boys were out of school yet.

"Oh, no, Miss; not for a quarter of an hour yet."

"Do you know if--if Master Charles Wardour is there to-day?" added Kate, with a gulp.

"I don't, Miss." And the woman looked hard at her.

"Do you know if any of them--any of them from St. James's, are in to- day?"

"No, Miss; I have not seen any of them, but very likely they may be. I saw Mr. Wardour go by yesterday morning."

So far they were all well, then; and Kate made her mind easier, and went on eating like a hungry child till the great clock struck four; when she hastily paid for her cakes and tarts, put on her gloves, and stood on the step, half in and half out of the shop, staring down the street. Out came the boys in a rush, making straight for the shop, and brushing past Kate; she, half alarmed, half affronted, descended from her post, still looking intently. Half a dozen more big fellows, eagerly talking, almost tumbled over her, and looked as if she had no business there; she seemed to be quite swept off the pavement into the street, and to be helpless in the midst of a mob, dashing around her. They might begin to tease her in a minute; and more terrified than at any moment of her journey, she was almost ready to cry, when the tones of a well-known voice came on her ear close to her--"I say, Will, you come and see my new terrier;" and before the words were uttered, with a cry of, "Charlie, Charlie!" she was clinging to a stout boy who had been passing without looking at her.

"Let go, I say. Who are you?" was the first rough greeting.

"O Charlie, Charlie!" almost sobbing, and still grasping his arm tight.

"Oh, I say!" and he stood with open mouth staring at her.

"O Charlie! take me home!"

"Yes, yes; come along!--Get off with you, fellows!" he added--turning round upon the other boys, who were beginning to stare--and exclaimed, "It's nothing but our Kate!"

Oh! what a thrill there was in hearing those words; and the boys, who were well-behaved and gentlemanly, were not inclined to molest her. So she hurried on, holding Charles's arm for several steps, till they were out of the hubbub, when he turned again and stared, and again exclaimed, "I say!" all that he could at present utter; and Kate looked at his ruddy face and curly head, and dusty coat and inky collar, as if she would eat him for very joy.

"I say!" and this time he really did say, "Where are the rest of them?"

"At home, aren't they?"

"What, didn't they bring you in?"

"Oh no!"

"Come, don't make a tomfoolery of it; that's enough. I shall have all the fellows at me for your coming up in that way, you know. Why couldn't you shake hands like anyone else?"

"O Charlie, I couldn't help it! Please let us go home!"

"Do you mean that you aren't come from there?"

"No," said Kate, half ashamed, but far more exultant, and hanging down her head; "I came from London--I came by myself. My aunt wanted me to tell a story, and--and I have run away. O Charlie! take me home!" and with a fresh access of alarm, she again threw her arms round him, as if to gain his protection from some enemy.

"Oh, I say!" again he cried, looking up the empty street and down again, partly for the enemy, partly to avoid eyes; but he only beheld three dirty children and an old woman, so he did not throw her off roughly. "Ran away!" and he gave a great whistle.

"Yes, yes. My aunt shut me up because I would not tell a story," said Kate, really believing it herself. "Oh, let us get home, Charlie, do."

"Very well, if you won't throttle a man; and let me get Tony in here," he added, going on a little way towards a small inn stable- yard.

"Oh, don't go," cried Kate, who, once more protected, could not bear to be left alone a moment; but Charlie plunged into the yard, and came back not only with the pony, but with a plaid, and presently managed to mount Kate upon the saddle, throwing the plaid round her so as to hide the short garments and long scarlet stockings, that were not adapted for riding, all with a boy's rough and tender care for the propriety of his sister's appearance.

"There, that will do," said he, holding the bridle. "So you found it poor fun being My Lady, and all that."

"Oh! it was awful, Charlie! You little know, in your peaceful retirement, what are the miseries of the great."

"Come, Kate, don't talk bosh out of your books. What did they do to you? They didn't lick you, did they?"

"No, no; nonsense," said Kate, rather affronted; "but they wanted to make me forget all that I cared for, and they really did shut me up because I said I would not write a falsehood to please them! They did, Charlie!" and her eyes shone.

"Well, I always knew they must be a couple of horrid old owls," began Charlie.

"Oh! I didn't mean Aunt Jane," said Kate, feeling a little compunction. "Ah!" with a start and scream, "who is coming?" as she heard steps behind them.

"You little donkey, you'll be off! Who should it be but Armyn?"

For Armyn generally overtook his brother on a Saturday, and walked home with him for the Sunday.

Charles hailed him with a loud "Hollo, Armyn! What d'ye think I've got here?"

"Kate! Why, how d'ye do! Why, they never told me you were coming to see us."

"They didn't know," whispered Kate.

"She's run away, like a jolly brick!" said Charlie, patting the pony vehemently as he made this most inappropriate comparison.

"Run away! You don't mean it!" cried Armyn, standing still and aghast, so much shocked that her elevation turned into shame; and Charles answered for her -

"Yes, to be sure she did, when they locked her up because she wouldn't tell lies to please them. How did you get out, Kittens? What jolly good fun it must have been!"

"Is this so, Kate?" said Armyn, laying his hand on the bridle; and his displeasure roused her spirit of self-defence, and likewise a sense of ill-usage.

"To be sure it is," she said, raising her head indignantly. "I would not be made to tell fashionable falsehoods; and so--and so I came home, for Papa to protect me:" and if she had not had to take care to steady herself on her saddle, she would have burst out sobbing with vexation at Armyn's manner.

"And no one knew you were coming?" said he.

"No, of course not; I slipped out while they were all in confabulation in Aunt Jane's room, and they were sure not to find me gone till dinner time, and if they are very cross, not then."

"You go on, Charlie," said Armyn, restoring the bridle to his brother; "I'll over-take you by the time you get home."

"What are you going to do?" cried boy and girl with one voice.

"Well, I suppose it is fair to tell you," said Armyn. "I must go and telegraph what is become of you."

There was a howl and a shriek at this. They would come after her and take her away, when she only wanted to be hid and kept safe; it was a cruel shame, and Charles was ready to fly at his brother and pommel him; indeed, Armyn had to hold him by one shoulder, and say in the voice that meant that he would be minded, "Steady, boy I--I'm very sorry, my little Katie; it's a melancholy matter, but you must have left those poor old ladies in a dreadful state of alarm about you, and they ought not to be kept in it!"

"Oh! but Armyn, Armyn, do only get home, and see what Papa says."

"I am certain what he will say, and it would only be the trouble of sending someone in, and keeping the poor women in a fright all the longer. Besides, depend on it, the way to have them sending down after you would be to say nothing. Now, if they hear you are safe, you are pretty secure of spending to-morrow at least with us. Let me go, Kate; it must be done. I cannot help it."

Even while he spoke, the kind way of crossing her will was so like home, that it gave a sort of happiness, and she felt she could not resist; so she gave a sigh, and he turned back.

How much of the joy and hope of her journey had he not carried away with him! His manner of treating her exploit made her even doubt how his father might receive it; and yet the sight of old scenes, and the presence of Charlie, was such exceeding delight, that it seemed to kill off all unpleasant fears or anticipations; and all the way home it was one happy chatter of inquiries for everyone, of bits of home news, and exclamations at the sight of some well-known tree, or the outline of a house remembered for some adventure; the darker the twilight the happier her tongue. The dull suburb, all little pert square red-brick houses, with slated roofs and fine names, in the sloppiness of a grey November day, was dear to Kate; every little shop window with the light streaming out was like a friend; and she anxiously gazed into the rough parties out for their Saturday purchases, intending to nod to anyone she might know, but it was too dark for recognitions; and when at length they passed the dark outline of the church, she was silent, her heart again bouncing as if it would beat away her breath and senses. The windows were dark; it was a sign that Evening Service was just over. The children turned in at the gate, just as Armyn overtook them. He lifted Kate off her pony. She could not have stood, but she could run, and she flew to the drawing-room. No one was there; perhaps she was glad. She knew the cousins would be dressing for tea, and in another moment she had torn open Sylvia's door.

Sylvia, who was brushing her hair, turned round. She stared--as if she had seen a ghost. Then the two children held out their arms, and rushed together with a wild scream that echoed through the house, and brought Mary flying out of her room to see who was hurt! and to find, rolling on her sister's bed, a thing that seemed to have two bodies and two faces glued together, four legs, and all its arms and hands wound round and round.

"Sylvia! What is it? Who is it? What is she doing to you?" began Mary; but before the words were out of her mouth, the thing had flown at her neck, and pulled her down too; and the grasp and the clinging and the kisses told her long before she had room or eyes or voice to know the creature by. A sort of sobbing out of each name between them was all that was heard at first.

At last, just as Mary was beginning to say, "My own own Katie! how did you come--" Mr. Wardour's voice on the stairs called "Mary!"

"Have you seen him, my dear?"

"No;" but Kate was afraid now she had heard his voice, for it was grave.

"Mary!" And Mary went. Kate sat up, holding Sylvia's hand.

They heard him ask, "Is Kate there?"

"Yes." And then there were lower voices that Kate could not hear, and which therefore alarmed her; and Sylvia, puzzled and frightened, sat holding her hand, listening silently.

Presently Mr. Wardour came in; and his look was graver than his tone; but it was so pitying, that in a moment Kate flew to his breast, and as he held her in his arms she cried, "O Papa! Papa! I have found you again! you will not turn me away."

"I must do whatever may be right, my dear child," said Mr. Wardour, holding her close, so that she felt his deep love, though it was not an undoubting welcome. "I will hear all about it when you have rested, and then I may know what is best to be done."

"Oh! keep me, keep me, Papa."

"You will be here to-morrow at least," he said, disengaging himself from her. "This is a terrible proceeding of yours, Kate, but it is no time for talking of it; and as your aunts know where you are, nothing more can be done at present; so we will wait to understand it till you are rested and composed."

He went away; and Kate remained sobered and confused, and Mary stood looking at her, sad and perplexed.

"O Kate! Kate!" she said, "what have you been doing?"

"What is the matter? Are not you glad?" cried Sylvia; and the squeeze of her hand restored Kate's spirits so much that she broke forth with her story, told in her own way, of persecution and escape, as she had wrought herself up to believe in it; and Sylvia clung to her, with flushed cheeks and ardent eyes, resenting every injury that her darling detailed, triumphing in her resistance, and undoubting that here she would be received and sheltered from all; while Mary, distressed and grieved, and cautioned by her father to take care not to show sympathy that might be mischievous, was carried along in spite of herself to admire and pity her child, and burn with indignation at such ill-treatment, almost in despair at the idea that the child must be sent back again, yet still not discarding that trust common to all Mr. Wardour's children, that "Papa would do ANYTHING to hinder a temptation."

And so, with eager words and tender hands, Kate was made ready for the evening meal, and went down, clinging on one side to Mary, on the other to Sylvia--a matter of no small difficulty on the narrow staircase, and almost leading to a general avalanche of young ladies, all upon the head of little Lily, who was running up to greet and be greeted, and was almost devoured by Kate when at length they did get safe downstairs.

It was a somewhat quiet, grave meal; Mr. Wardour looked so sad and serious, that all felt that it would not do to indulge in joyous chatter, and the little girls especially were awed; though through all there was a tender kindness in his voice and look, whenever he did but offer a slice of bread to his little guest, such as made her feel what was home and what was love--"like a shower of rain after a parched desert" as she said to herself; and she squeezed Sylvia's hand under the table whenever she could.

Mr. Wardour spoke to her very little. He said he had seen Colonel Umfraville's name in the Gazette, and asked about his coming home; and when she had answered that the time and speed of the journey were to depend on Giles's health, he turned from her to Armyn, and began talking to him about some public matters that seemed very dull to Kate; and one little foolish voice within her said, "He is not like Mrs. George Wardour, he forgets what I am;" but there was a wiser, more loving voice to answer, "Dear Papa, he thinks of me as myself; he is no respecter of persons. Oh, I hope he is not angry with me!"

When tea was over Mr. Wardour stood up, and said, "I shall wish you children good-night now; I have to read with John Bailey for his Confirmation, and to prepare for to-morrow;--and you, Kate, must go to bed early.--Mary, she had better sleep with you."

This was rather a blank, for sleeping with Sylvia again had been Kate's dream of felicity; yet this was almost lost in the sweetness of once more coming in turn for the precious kiss and good-night, in the midst of which she faltered, "O Papa, don't be angry with me!"

"I am not angry, Katie," he said gently; "I am very sorry. You have done a thing that nothing can justify, and that may do you much future harm; and I cannot receive you as if you had come properly. I do not know what excuse there was for you, and I cannot attend to you to-night; indeed, I do not think you could tell me rightly; but another time we will talk it all over, and I will try to help you. Now good-night, my dear child."

Those words of his, "I will try to help you," were to Kate like a promise of certain rescue from all her troubles; and, elastic ball that her nature was, no sooner was his anxious face out of sight, and she secure that he was not angry, than up bounded her spirits again. She began wondering why Papa thought she could not tell him properly, and forthwith began to give what she intended for a full and particular history of all that she had gone through.

It was a happy party round the fire; Kate and Sylvia both together in the large arm-chair, and Lily upon one of its arms; Charles in various odd attitudes before the fire; Armyn at the table with his book, half reading, half listening; Mary with her work; and Kate pouring out her story, making herself her own heroine, and describing her adventures, her way of life, and all her varieties of miseries, in the most glowing colours. How she did rattle on! It would be a great deal too much to tell; indeed it would be longer than this whole story!

Sylvia and Charlie took it all in, pitied, wondered, and were indignant, with all their hearts; indeed Charlie was once heard to wish he could only get that horrid old witch near the horse-pond; and when Kate talked of her Diana face, he declared that he should get the old brute of a cat into the field, and set all the boys to stone her.

Little Lily listened, not sure whether it was not all what she called "a made-up story only for prettiness;" and Mary, sitting over her work, was puzzled, and saw that her father was right in saying that Kate could not at present give an accurate account of herself. Mary knew her truthfulness, and that she would not have said what she knew to be invention; but those black eyes, glowing like little hot coals, and those burning cheeks, as well as the loud, squeaky key of the voice, all showed that she had worked herself up into a state of excitement, such as not to know what was invented by an exaggerating memory. Besides, it could not be all true; it did not agree; the ill-treatment was not consistent with the grandeur. For Kate had taken to talking very big, as if she was an immensely important personage, receiving much respect wherever she went; and though Armyn once or twice tried putting in a sober matter-of-fact question for the fun of disconcerting her, she was too mad to care or understand what he said.

"Oh no! she never was allowed to do anything for herself. That was quite a rule, and very tiresome it was."

"Like the King of Spain, you can't move your chair away from the fire without the proper attendant."

"I never do put on coals or wood there!"

"There may be several reasons for that," said Armyn, recollecting how nearly Kate had once burnt the house down.

"Oh, I assure you it would not do for me," said Kate. "If it were not so inconvenient in that little house, I should have my own man- servant to attend to my fire, and walk out behind me. Indeed, now Perkins always does walk behind me, and it is such a bore."

And what was the consequence of all this wild chatter? When Mary had seen the hot-faced eager child into bed, she came down to her brother in the drawing-room with her eyes brimful of tears, saying, "Poor dear child! I am afraid she is very much spoilt!"

"Don't make up your mind to-night," said Armyn. "She is slightly insane as yet! Never mind, Mary; her heart is in the right place, if her head is turned a little."

"It is very much turned indeed," said Mary. "How wise it was of Papa not to let Sylvia sleep with her! What will he do with her? Oh dear!"

CHAPTER XIII.

The Sunday at Oldburgh was not spent as Kate would have had it. It dawned upon her in the midst of horrid dreams, ending by wakening to an overpowering sick headache, the consequence of the agitations and alarms of the previous day, and the long fast, appeased by the contents of the pastry-cook's shop, with the journey and the excitement of the meeting--altogether quite sufficient to produce such a miserable feeling of indisposition, that if Kate could have thought at all of anything but present wretchedness, she would have feared that she was really carrying out the likeness to Cardinal Wolsey by laying her bones among them.

That it was not quite so bad as that, might be inferred from her having no doctor but Mary Wardour, who attended to her most assiduously from her first moans at four o'clock in the morning, till her dropping off to sleep about noon; when the valiant Mary, in the absence of everyone at church, took upon herself to pen a note, to catch the early Sunday post, on her own responsibility, to Lady Barbara Umfraville, to say that her little cousin was so unwell that it would be impossible to carry out the promise of bringing her home on Monday, which Mr. Wardour had written on Saturday night.

Sleep considerably repaired her little ladyship; and when she had awakened, and supped up a bason of beef-tea, toast and all, with considerable appetite, she was so much herself again, that there was no reason that anyone should be kept at home to attend to her. Mary's absence was extremely inconvenient, as she was organist and leader of the choir.

"So, Katie dear," she said, when she saw her patient on her legs again, making friends with the last new kitten of the old cat, "you will not mind being left alone, will you? It is only for the Litany and catechising, you know."

Kate looked blank, and longed to ask that Sylvia might stay with her, but did not venture; knowing that she was not ill enough for it to be a necessity, and that no one in that house was ever kept from church, except for some real and sufficient cause.

But the silly thoughts that passed through the little head in the hour of solitude would fill two or three volumes. In the first place, she was affronted. They made very little of her, considering who she was, and how she had come to see them at all risks, and how ill she had been! They would hardly have treated a little village child so negligently as their visitor, the Countess -

Then her heart smote her. She remembered Mary's tender and assiduous nursing all the morning, and how she had already stayed from service and Sunday school; and she recollected her honour for her friends for not valuing her for her rank; and in that mood she looked out the Psalms and Lessons, which she had not been able to read in the morning, and when she had finished them, began to examine the book- case in search of a new, or else a very dear old, Sunday book.

But then something went "crack,"--or else it was Kate's fancy--for she started as if it had been a cannon-ball; and though she sat with her book in her lap by the fire in Mary's room, all the dear old furniture and pictures round her, her head was weaving an unheard-of imagination, about robbers coming in rifling everything--coming up the stairs--creak, creak, was that their step?--she held her breath, and her eyes dilated--seizing her for the sake of her watch! What article there would be in the paper--"Melancholy disappearance of the youthful Countess of Caergwent." Then Aunt Barbara would be sorry she had treated her so cruelly; then Mary would know she ought not to have abandoned the child who had thrown herself on her protection.

That was the way Lady Caergwent spent her hour. She had been kidnapped and murdered a good many times before; there was a buzz in the street, her senses came back, and she sprang out on the stairs to meet her cousins, calling herself quite well again. And then they had a very peaceful, pleasant time; she was one of them again, when, as of old, Mr. Wardour came into the drawing-room, and she stood up with Charles, Sylvia, and little Lily, who was now old enough for the Catechism, and then the Collect, and a hymn. Yes, she had Collect and hymn ready too, and some of the Gospel; Aunt Barbara always heard her say them on Sunday, besides some very difficult questions, not at all like what Mr. Wardour asked out of his own head.

Kate was a little afraid he would make his teaching turn on submitting to rulers; it was an Epistle that would have given him a good opportunity, for it was the Fourth Epiphany Sunday, brought in at the end of the Sundays after Trinity. If he made his teaching personal, something within her wondered if she could bear it, and was ready to turn angry and defiant. But no such thing; what he talked to them about was the gentle Presence that hushed the waves and winds in outward nature, and calmed the wild spiritual torments of the possessed; and how all fears and terrors, all foolish fancies and passionate tempers, will be softened into peace when the thought of Him rises in the heart.

Kate wondered if she should be able to think of that next time she was going to work herself into an agony.

But at present all was like a precious dream, to be enjoyed as slowly as the moments could be persuaded to pass. Out came the dear old Dutch Bible History, with pictures of everything--pictures that they had looked at every Sunday since they could walk, and could have described with their eyes shut; and now Kate was to feast her eyes once again upon them, and hear how many little Lily knew; and a pretty sight it was, that tiny child, with her fat hands clasped behind her so as not to be tempted to put a finger on the print, going so happily and thoroughly through all the creatures that came to Adam to be named, and showing the whole procession into the Ark, and, her favourite of all, the Angels coming down to Jacob.

Then came tea; and then Kate was pronounced, to her great delight, well enough for Evening Service. The Evening Service she always thought a treat, with the lighted church, and the choicest singing-- the only singing that had ever taken hold of Kate's tuneless ear, and that seemed to come home to her. At least, to-night it came home as it had never done before; it seemed to touch some tender spot in her heart, and when she thought how dear it was, and how little she had cared about it, and how glad she had been to go away, she found the candles dancing in a green mist, and great drops came down upon the Prayer-book in her hand.

Then it could not be true that she had no feeling. She was crying-- the first time she had ever known herself cry except for pain or at reproof; and she was really so far pleased, that she made no attempt to stop the great tears that came trickling down at each familiar note, at each thought how long it had been since she had heard them. She cried all church time; for whenever she tried to attend to the prayers, the very sound of the voice she loved so well set her off again; and Sylvia, tenderly laying a hand on her by way of sympathy, made her weep the more, though still so softly and gently that it was like a strange sort of happiness--almost better than joy and merriment. And then the sermon--upon the text, "Peace, be still,"-- was on the same thought on which her uncle had talked to the children: not that she followed it much; the very words "peace" and "be still," seemed to be enough to touch, soften, and dissolve her into those sweet comfortable tears.

Perhaps they partly came from the weakening of the morning's indisposition; at any rate, when she moved, after the Blessing, holding the pitying Sylvia's hand, she found that she was very much tired, her eyelids were swollen and aching, and in fact she was fit for nothing but bed, where Mary and Sylvia laid her; and she slept, and slept in dreamless soundness, till she was waked by Mary's getting up in the morning, and found herself perfectly well.

"And now, Sylvia," she said, as they went downstairs hand-in-hand, "let us put it all out of our heads, and try and think all day that it is just one of our old times, and that I am your old Kate. Let me do my lessons and go into school, and have some fun, and quite forget all that is horrid."

But there was something to come before this happy return to old times. As soon as breakfast was over Mr Wardour said, "Now, Kate, I want you." And then she knew what was coming; and somehow, she did not feel exactly the same about her exploit and its causes by broad daylight, now that she was cool. Perhaps she would have been glad to hang back; yet on the whole, she had a great deal to say to "Papa," and it was a relief, though rather terrific, to find herself alone with him in the study.

"Now, Kate," said he again, with his arm round her, as she stood by him, "will you tell me what led you to this very sad and strange proceeding?"

Kate hung her head, and ran her fingers along the mouldings of his chair.

"Why was it, my dear?" asked Mr. Wardour.

"It was--" and she grew bolder at the sound of her own voice, and more confident in the goodness of her cause--"it was because Aunt Barbara said I must write what was not true, and--and I'll never tell a falsehood--never, for no one!" and her eyes flashed.

"Gently, Kate," he said, laying his hand upon hers; "I don't want to know what you never WILL do, only what you have done. What was this falsehood?"

"Why, Papa, the other Sylvia--Sylvia Joanna, you know--has her birthday to-day, and we settled at Bournemouth that I should spend the day with her; and on Saturday, when Aunt Barbara heard of it, she said she did not want me to be intimate there, and that I must not go, and told me to write a note to say she had made a previous engagement for me."

"And do you know that she had not done so?"

"O Papa! she could not; for when I said I would not write a lie, she never said it was true."

"Was that what you said to your aunt?"

"Yes,"--and Kate hung her head--"I was in a passion."

"Then, Kate, I do not wonder that Lady Barbara insisted on obedience, instead of condescending to argue with a child who could be so insolent."

"But, Papa," said Kate, abashed for a moment, then getting eager, "she does tell fashionable falsehoods; she says she is not at home when she is, and--"

"Stay, Kate; it is not for you to judge of grown people's doings. Neither I nor Mary would like to use that form of denying ourselves; but it is usually understood to mean only not ready to receive visitors. In the same way, this previous engagement was evidently meant to make the refusal less discourteous, and you were not even certain it did not exist."

"My Italian mistress did want to come on Monday," faltered Kate, "but it was not 'previous.'"

"Then, Kate, who was it that went beside the mark in letting us believe that Lady Barbara locked you up to make you tell falsehoods?"

"Indeed, Papa, I did not say locked--Charlie and Sylvia said that."

"But did you correct them?"

"O Papa, I did not mean it! But I am naughty now! I always am naughty, so much worse than I used to be at home. Indeed I am, and I never do get into a good vein now. O Papa, Papa, can't you get me out of it all? If you could only take me home again! I don't think my aunts want to keep me--they say I am so bad and horrid, and that I make Aunt Jane ill. Oh, take me back, Papa!"

He did take her on his knee, and held her close to him. "I wish I could, my dear," he said; "I should like to have you again! but it cannot be. It is a different state of life that has been appointed for you; and you would not be allowed to make your home with me, with no older a person than Mary to manage for you. If your aunt had not been taken from us, then--" and Kate ventured to put her arm round his neck--"then this would have been your natural home; but as things are with us, I could not make my house such as would suit the requirements of those who arrange for you. And, my poor child, I fear we let the very faults spring up that are your sorrow now."

"Oh no, no, Papa, you helped me! Aunt Barbara only makes me--oh! may I say?--hate her! for indeed there is no helping it! I can't be good there."

"What is it? What do you mean, my dear? What is your difficulty? And I will try to help you."

Poor Kate found it not at all easy to explain when she came to particulars. "Always cross," was the clearest idea in her mind; "never pleased with her, never liking anything she did--not punishing, but much worse." She had not made out her case, she knew; but she could only murmur again, "It all went wrong, and I was very unhappy."

Mr. Wardour sighed from the bottom of his heart; he was very sorrowful, too, for the child that was as his own. And then he went back and thought of his early college friend, and of his own wife who had so fondled the little orphan--all that was left of her sister. It was grievous to him to put that child away from him when she came clinging to him, and saying she was unhappy, and led into faults.

"It will be better when your uncle comes home," he began.

"Oh no, Papa, indeed it will not. Uncle Giles is more stern than Aunt Barbara. Aunt Jane says it used to make her quite unhappy to see how sharp he was with poor Giles and Frank."

"I never saw him in his own family," said Mr. Wardour thoughtfully; "but this I know, Kate, that your father looked up to him, young as he then was, more than to anyone; that he was the only person among them all who ever concerned himself about you or your mother; and that on the two occasions when I saw him, I thought him very like your father."

"I had rather he was like you, Papa," sighed Kate. "Oh, if I was but your child!"

she added, led on by a little involuntary pressure of his encircling arm.

"Don't let us talk of what is not, but of what is," said Mr. Wardour; "let us try to look on things in their right light. It has been the will of Heaven to call you, my little girl, to a station where you will, if you live, have many people's welfare depending on you, and your example will be of weight with many. You must go through training for it, and strict training may be the best for you. Indeed, it must be the best, or it would not have been permitted to befall you."

"But it does not make me good, it makes me naughty."

"No, Kate; nothing, nobody can make you naughty; nothing is strong enough to do that."

Kate knew what he meant, and hung her head.

"My dear, I do believe that you feel forlorn and dreary, and miss the affection you have had among us; but have you ever thought of the Friend who is closest of all to us, and who is especially kind to a fatherless child?"

"I can't--I can't feel it--Papa, I can't. And then, why was it made so that I must go away from you and all?"

"You will see some day, though you cannot see now, my dear. If you use it rightly, you will feel the benefit. Meantime, you must take it on trust, just as you do my love for you, though I am going to carry you back."

"Yes; but I can feel you loving me."

"My dear child, it only depends on yourself to feel your Heavenly Father loving you. If you will set yourself to pray with your heart, and think of His goodness to you, and ask Him for help and solace in all your present vexatious and difficulties, never mind how small, you WILL become conscious of his tender pity and love to you."

"Ah! but I am not good!"

"But He can make you so, Kate. Your have been wearied by religious teaching hitherto, have you not?"

"Except when it was pretty and like poetry," whispered Kate.

"Put your heart to your prayers now, Kate. Look in the Psalms for verses to suit your loneliness; recollect that you meet us in spirit when you use the same Prayers, read the same Lessons, and think of each other. Or, better still, carry your troubles to Him; and when you HAVE felt His help, you will know what that is far better than I can tell you."

Kate only answered with a long breath; not feeling as if she could understand such comfort, but with a resolve to try.

"And now," said Mr. Wardour, "I must take you home to-morrow, and I will speak for you to Lady Barbara, and try to obtain her forgiveness; but, Kate, I do not think you quite understand what a shocking proceeding this was of yours."

"I know it was wrong to fancy THAT, and say THAT about Aunt Barbara. I'll tell her so," said Kate, with a trembling voice.

"Yes, that will be right; but it was this--this expedition that I meant."

"It was coming to you, Papa!"

"Yes, Kate; but did you think what an outrageous act it was? There is something particularly grievous in a little girl, or a woman of any age, casting off restraint, and setting out in the world unprotected and contrary to authority. Do you know, it frightened me so much, that till I saw more of you I did not like you to be left alone with Sylvia."

The deep red colour flushed all over Kate's face and neck in her angry shame and confusion, burning darker and more crimson, so that Mr. Wardour was very sorry for her, and added, "I am obliged to say this, because you ought to know that it is both very wrong in itself, and will be regarded by other people as more terrible than what you are repenting of more. So, if you do find yourself distrusted and in disgrace, you must not think it unjust and cruel, but try to submit patiently, and learn not to be reckless and imprudent. My poor child, I wish you could have so come to us that we might have been happier together. Perhaps you will some day; and in the meantime, if you have any troubles, or want to know anything, you may always write to me."

"Writing is not speaking," said Kate ruefully.

"No; but it comes nearer to it as people get older. Now go, my dear; I am busy, and you had better make the most of your time with your cousins."

Kate's heart was unburthened now; and though there was much alarm, pain, and grief, in anticipation, yet she felt more comfortable in herself than she had done for months. "Papa" had never been so tender with her, and she knew that he had forgiven her. She stept back to the drawing-room, very gentle and subdued, and tried to carry out her plans of living one of her old days, by beginning with sharing the lessons as usual, and then going out with her cousins to visit the school, and see some of the parishioners. It was very nice and pleasant; she was as quiet and loving as possible, and threw herself into all the dear old home matters. It was as if for a little while Katharine was driven out of Katharine, and a very sweet little maiden left instead--thinking about other things and people instead of herself, and full of affection and warmth. The improvement that the half year's discipline had made in her bearing and manners was visible now; her uncouth abrupt ways were softened, though still she felt that the naturally gentle and graceful Sylvia would have made a better countess than she did.

They spent the evening in little tastes of all their favourite drawing-room games, just for the sake of having tried them once more; and Papa himself came in and took a share--a very rare treat;--and he always thought of such admirable things in "Twenty questions," and made "What's my thought like ?" more full of fun than anyone.

It was a very happy evening--one of the most happy that Kate had ever passed. She knew HOW to enjoy her friends now, and how precious they were to her; and she was just so much tamed by the morning's conversation, and by the dread of the future, as not to be betrayed into dangerously high spirits. That loving, pitying way of Mary's, and her own Sylvia's exceeding pleasure in having her, were delightful; and all through she felt the difference between the real genuine love that she could rest on, and the mere habit of fondling of the other Sylvia.

"O Sylvia," she said, as they walked upstairs, hand in hand, pausing on every stop to make it longer, "how could I be so glad to go away before?"

"We didn't know," said Sylvia.

"No," as they crept up another step; "Sylvia, will you always think of me just here on this step, as you go up to bed?"

"Yes," said Sylvia, "that I will. And, Katie, would it be wrong just to whisper a little prayer then that you might be good and happy?"

"It couldn't be wrong, Sylvia; only couldn't you just ask, too, for me to come home?"

"I don't know," said Sylvia thoughtfully, pausing a long time on the step. "You see we know it is sure to be God's will that you should be good and happy; but if it was not for you to come home, we might be like Balaam, you know, if we asked it too much, and it might come about in some terrible way."

"I didn't think of that," said Kate. And the two little girls parted gravely and peacefully; Kate somehow feeling as if, though grievous things were before her, the good little kind Sylvia's hearty prayers must obtain some good for her.

There is no use in telling how sad the parting was when Mr. Wardour and the little Countess set out for London again. Mary had begged hard to go too, thinking that she could plead for Kate better than anyone else; but Mr. Wardour thought Lady Barbara more likely to be angered than softened by their clinging to their former charge; and besides, it was too great an expense.

He had no doubt of Lady Barbara's displeasure from the tone of the note that morning received, coldly thanking him and Miss Wardour for their intelligence, and his promise to restore Lady Caergwent on Tuesday. She was sorry to trouble him to bring the child back; she would have come herself, but that her sister was exceedingly unwell, from the alarm coming at a time of great family affliction. If Lady Caergwent were not able to return on Tuesday, she would send down her own maid to bring her home on Wednesday. The letter was civility itself; but it was plain that Lady Barbara thought Kate's illness no better than the "previous engagement," in the note that never was written.

What was the family affliction? Kate could not guess, but was inclined to imagine privately that Aunt Barbara was magnifying Uncle Giles's return without being a General into a family affliction, on purpose to aggravate her offence. However, in the train, Mr. Wardour, who had been looking at the Supplement of the Times, lent to him by a fellow-traveller, touched her, and made her read -

"On the 11th, at Alexandria, in his 23rd year, Lieutenant Giles de la Poer Umfraville, of the 109th regiment; eldest, and last survivor of the children of the Honourable Giles Umfraville, late Lieutenant- Colonel of the 109th regiment."

Kate knew she ought to be very sorry, and greatly pity the bereaved father and mother; but, somehow, she could not help dwelling most upon the certainty that everyone would be much more hard upon her, and cast up this trouble to her, as if she had known of it, and run away on purpose to make it worse. It must have been this that they were talking about in Aunt Jane's room, and this must have made them so slow to detect her flight.

In due time the train arrived, a cab was taken, and Kate, beginning to tremble with fright, sat by Mr. Wardour, and held his coat as if clinging to him as long as she could was a comfort. Sometimes she wished the cab would go faster, so that it might be over; sometimes-- especially when the streets became only too well known to her--she wished that they would stretch out and out for ever, that she might still be sitting by Papa, holding his coat. It seemed as if that would be happiness enough for life!

Here was Bruton Street; here the door that on Saturday had shut behind her! It was only too soon open, and Kate kept her eyes on the ground, ashamed that even the butler should see her. She hung back, waiting till Mr. Wardour had paid the cabman; but there was no spinning it out, she had to walk upstairs, her only comfort being that her hand was in his.

No one was in the drawing-room; but before long Lady Barbara came in. Kate durst not look up at her, but was sure, from the tone of her voice, that she must have her very sternest face; and there was something to make one shiver in the rustle of her silk dress as she curtsied to Mr. Wardour.

"I have brought home my little niece," he said, drawing Kate forward; "and I think I may truly say, that she is very sorry for what has passed."

There was a pause; Kate knew the terrible black eyes were upon her, but she felt, besides, the longing to speak out the truth, and a sense that with Papa by her side she had courage to do so.

"I am sorry, Aunt Barbara," she said; "I was very self-willed; I ought not to have fancied things, nor said you used me ill, and wanted me to tell stories."

Kate's heart was lighter; though it beat so terribly as she said those words. She knew that they pleased ONE of the two who were present, and she knew they were right.

"It is well you should be so far sensible of your misconduct," said Lady Barbara; but her voice was as dry and hard as ever, and Mr. Wardour added, "She is sincerely sorry; it is from her voluntary confession that I know how much trouble she has given you; and I think, if you will kindly forgive her, that you will find her less self-willed in future."

And he shoved Kate a little forward, squeezing her hand, and trying to withdraw his own. She perceived that he meant that she ought to ask pardon; and though it went against her more than her first speech had done, she contrived to say, "I do beg pardon, Aunt Barbara; I will try to do better."

"My pardon is one thing, Katharine," said Lady Barbara. "If your sorrow is real, of course I forgive you;" and she took Kate's right- hand--the left was still holding by the fingers' ends to Mr. Wardour. "But the consequences of such behaviour are another consideration. My personal pardon cannot, and ought not, to avert them--as I am sure you must perceive, Mr. Wardour," she added, as the frightened child retreated upon him. Those consequences of Aunt Barbara's were fearful things! Mr. Wardour said something, to which Kate scarcely attended in her alarm, and her aunt went on -

"For Lady Caergwent's own sake, I shall endeavour to keep this most unfortunate step as much a secret as possible. I believe that scarcely anyone beyond this house is aware of it; and I hope that your family will perceive the necessity of being equally cautious."

Mr. Wardour bowed, and assented.

"But," added Lady Barbara, "it has made it quite impossible for my sister and myself to continue to take the charge of her. My sister's health has suffered from the constant noise and restlessness of a child in the house: the anxiety and responsibility are far too much for her; and in addition to this, she had such severe nervous seizures from the alarm of my niece's elopement, that nothing would induce me to subject her to a recurrence of such agitation. We must receive the child for the present, of course; but as soon as my brother returns, and can attend to business, the matter must be referred to the Lord Chancellor, and an establishment formed, with a lady at the head, who may have authority and experience to deal with such an ungovernable nature."

"Perhaps," said Mr. Wardour, "under these circumstances it might be convenient for me to take her home again for the present."

Kate quivered with hope; but that was far too good to be true; Lady Barbara gave a horrid little cough, and there was a sound almost of offence in her "Thank you, you are very kind, but that would be quite out of the question. I am at present responsible for my niece."

"I thought, perhaps," said Mr. Wardour, as an excuse for the offer, "that as Lady Jane is so unwell, and Colonel Umfraville in so much affliction, it might be a relief to part with her at present."

"Thank you," again said Lady Barbara, as stiffly as if her throat were lined with whalebone; "no inconvenience can interfere with my duty."

Mr. Wardour knew there was no use in saying any more, and inquired after Lady Jane. She had, it appeared, been very ill on Saturday evening, and had not since left her room. Mr. Wardour then said that Kate had not been aware, till a few hours ago, of the death of her cousin, and inquired anxiously after the father and mother; but Lady Barbara would not do more than answer direct questions, and only said that her nephew had been too much weakened to bear the journey, and had sunk suddenly at Alexandria, and that his father was, she feared, very unwell. She could not tell how soon he was likely to be in England. Then she thanked Mr. Wardour for having brought Lady Caergwent home, and offered him some luncheon; but in such a grave grand way, that it was plain that she did not want him to eat it, and, feeling that he could do no more good, he kissed poor Kate and wished Lady Barbara good-bye.

Poor Kate stood, drooping, too much constrained by dismay even to try to cling to him, or run after him to the foot of the stairs.

"Now, Katharine," said her aunt, "come up with me to your Aunt Jane's room. She has been so much distressed about you, that she will not be easy till she has seen you."

Kate followed meekly; and found Aunt Jane sitting by the fire in her own room, looking flushed, hot, and trembling. She held out her arms, and Kate ran into them; but neither of them dared to speak, and Lady Barbara stood up, saying, "She says she is very sorry, and thus we may forgive her; as I know you do all the suffering you have undergone on her account."

Lady Jane held the child tighter, and Kate returned her kisses with all her might; but the other aunt said, "That will do. She must not be too much for you again." And they let go as if a cold wind had blown between them.

"Did Mr. Wardour bring her home?" asked Lady Jane.

"Yes; and was kind enough to propose taking her back again," was the answer, with a sneer, that made Kate feel desperately angry, though she did not understand it.

In truth, Lady Barbara was greatly displeased with the Wardours. She had always been led to think her niece's faults the effect of their management; and she now imagined that there had been some encouragement of the child's discontent to make her run away; and that if they had been sufficiently shocked and concerned, the truant would have been brought home much sooner. It all came of her having allowed her niece to associate with those children at Bournemouth. She would be more careful for the future.

Careful, indeed, she was! She had come to think of her niece as a sort of small wild beast that must never be let out of sight of some trustworthy person, lest she should fly away again.

A daily governess, an elderly person, very grave and silent, came in directly after breakfast, walked with the Countess, and heard the lessons; and after her departure, Kate was always to be in the room with her aunts, and never was allowed to sit in the schoolroom and amuse herself alone; but her tea was brought into the dining-room while her aunts were at dinner, and morning, noon, and night, she knew that she was being watched.

It was very bitter to her. It seemed to take all the spirit away from her, as if she did not care for books, lessons, or anything else. Sometimes her heart burnt with hot indignation, and she would squeeze her hands together, or wring round her handkerchief in a sort of misery; but it never got beyond that; she never broke out, for she was depressed by what was still worse, the sense of shame. Lady Barbara had not said many words, but had made her feel, in spite of having forgiven her, that she had done a thing that would be a disgrace to her for ever; a thing that would make people think twice before they allowed their children to associate with her; and that put her below the level of other girls. The very pain that Lady Barbara took to hush it up, her fears lest it should come to the ears of the De la Poers, her hopes that it MIGHT not be necessary to reveal it to her brother, assisted to weigh down Kate with a sense of the heinousness of what she had done, and sunk her so that she had no inclination to complain of the watchfulness around her. And Aunt Jane's sorrowful kindness went to her heart.

"How COULD you do it, my dear?" she said, in such a wonderful wistful tone, when Kate was alone with her.

Kate hung her head. She could not think now.

"It is so sad," added Lady Jane; "I hoped we might have gone on so nicely together. And now I hope your Uncle Giles will not hear of it. He would be so shocked, and never trust you again."

"YOU will trust me, when I have been good a long time, Aunt Jane?"

"My dear, I would trust you any time, you know; but then that's no use. I can't judge; and your Aunt Barbara says, after such lawlessness, you need very experienced training to root out old associations."

Perhaps the aunts were more shocked than was quite needful and treated Kate as if she had been older and known better what she was doing; but they were sincere in their horror at her offence; and once she even heard Lady Barbara saying to Mr. Mercer that there seemed to be a doom on the family--in the loss of the promising young man--and- -The words were not spoken, but Kate knew that she was this greatest of all misfortunes to the family.

Poor child! In the midst of all this, there was one comfort. She had not put aside what Mr. Wardour had told her about the Comforter she could always have. She DID say her prayers as she had never said them before, and she looked out in the Psalms and Lessons for comforting verses. She knew she had done very wrong, and she asked with all the strength of her heart to be forgiven, and made less unhappy, and that people might be kinder to her. Sometimes she thought no help was coming, and that her prayers did no good, but she went on; and then, perhaps, she got a kind little caress from Lady Jane, or Mr. Mercer spoke good-naturedly to her, or Lady Barbara granted her some little favour, and she felt as if there was hope and things were getting better; and she took courage all the more to pray that Uncle Giles might not be very hard upon her, nor the Lord Chancellor very cruel.

CHAPTER XIV.

A fortnight had passed, and had seemed nearly as long as a year, since Kate's return from Oldburgh, when one afternoon, when she was lazily turning over the leaves of a story-book that she knew so well by heart that she could go over it in the twilight, she began to gather from her aunt's words that somebody was coming.

They never told her anything direct; but by listening a little more attentively to what they were saying, she found out that a letter-- no, a telegram--had come while she was at her lessons; that Aunt Barbara had been taking rooms at a hotel; that she was insisting that Jane should not imagine they would come to-night--they would not come till the last train, and then neither of them would be equal -

"Poor dear Emily! But could we not just drive to the hotel and meet them? It will be so dreary for them."

"You go out at night! and for such a meeting! when you ought to be keeping yourself as quiet as possible! No, depend upon it they will prefer getting in quietly, and resting to-night; and Giles, perhaps, will step in to breakfast in the morning."

"And then you will bring him up to me at once! I wonder if the boy is much altered!"

Throb! throb! throb! went Kate's heart! So the terrible stern uncle was in England, and this was the time for her to be given up to the Lord Chancellor and all his myrmidons (a word that always came into her head when she was in a fright). She had never loved Aunt Jane so well; she almost loved Aunt Barbara, and began to think of clinging to her with an eloquent speech, pleading to be spared from the Lord Chancellor!

To-morrow morning--that was a respite!

There was a sound of wheels. Lady Jane started.

"They are giving a party next door," said Lady Barbara.

But the bell rang.

"Only a parcel coming home," said Lady Barbara. "Pray do not be nervous, Jane."

But the red colour was higher in Barbara's own cheeks, as there were steps on the stairs; and in quite a triumphant voice the butler announced, as he opened the door, "Colonel and Mrs. Umfraville!"

Kate stood up, and backed. It was Aunt Barbara's straight, handsome, terrible face, and with a great black moustache to make it worse. She saw that, and it was all she feared! She was glad the sofa was between them!

There was a lady besides all black bonnet and cloak; and there was a confusion of sounds, a little half sobbing of Aunt Jane's; but the other sister and the brother were quite steady and grave. It was his keen dark eye, sparkling like some wild animal's in the firelight, as Kate thought, which spied her out; and his deep grave voice said, "My little niece," as he held out his hand.

"Come and speak to your uncle, Katharine," said Lady Barbara; and not only had she to put her hand into that great firm one, but her forehead was scrubbed by his moustache. She had never been kissed by a moustache before, and she shuddered as if it had been on a panther's lip.

But then he said, "There, Emily;" and she found herself folded up in such arms as had never been round her before, with the very sweetest of kisses on her cheeks, the very kindest of eyes, full of moisture, gazing at her as if they had been hungry for her. Even when the embrace was over, the hand still held hers; and as she stood by the new aunt, a thought crossed her that had never come before, "I wonder if my mamma was like this!"

There was some explanation of how the travellers had come on, &c., and it was settled that they were to stay to dinner; after which Mrs. Umfraville went away with Lady Barbara to take off her bonnet.

Colonel Umfraville came and sat down by his sister on the sofa, and said, "Well Jane, how have you been?"

"Oh! much as usual:" and then there was a silence, till she moved a little nearer to him, put her hand on his arm, looked up in his face with swimming eyes, and said, "O Giles! Giles!"

He took her hand, and bent over her, saying, in the same grave steady voice, "Do not grieve for us, Jane. We have a great deal to be thankful for, and we shall do very well."

It made that loving tender-hearted Aunt Jane break quite down, cling to him and sob, "O Giles--those dear noble boys--how little we thought--and dear Caergwent too--and you away from home!"

She was crying quite violently, so as to be shaken by the sobs; and her brother stood over her, saying a kind word or two now and then, to try to soothe her; while Kate remained a little way off, with her black eyes wide open, thinking her uncle's face was almost displeased--at any rate, very rigid. He looked up at Kate, and signed towards a scent-bottle on the table. Kate gave it; and then, as if the movement had filled her with a panic, she darted out of the room, and flew up to the bedrooms, crying out, "Aunt Barbara, Aunt Jane is crying so terribly!"

"She will have one of her attacks! Oh!" began Lady Barbara, catching up a bottle of salvolatile.

"Had we not better leave her and Giles to one another?" said the tones that Kate liked so much.

"Oh! my dear, you don't know what these attacks are!" and away hurried Lady Barbara.

The bonnet was off now, leaving only a little plain net cap under it, round the calm gentle face. There was a great look of sadness, and the eyelids were heavy and drooping; but there was something that put Kate in mind of a mother dove in the softness of the large tender embrace, and the full sweet caressing tone. What a pity that such an aunt must know that she was an ill-behaved child, a misfortune to her lineage! She stood leaning against the door, very awkward and conscious. Mrs. Umfraville turned round, after smoothing her hair at the glass, smiled, and said, "I thought I should find you here, my little niece. You are Kate, I think."

"I used to be, but my aunts here call me Katharine."

"Is this your little room?" said Mrs. Umfraville, as they came out. The fact was, that she thought the sisters might be happier with their brother if she delayed a little; so she came into Kate's room, and was beginning to look at her books, when Lady Barbara came hurrying up again.

"She is composed now, Emily. Oh! it is all right; I did not know where Katharine might be."

Kate's colour glowed. She could not bear that this sweet Aunt Emily should guess that she was a state prisoner, kept in constant view.

Lady Jane was quiet again, and nothing more that could overthrow her spirits passed all the evening; there was only a little murmur of talk, generally going on chiefly between Lady Barbara and Mrs. Umfraville, though occasionally the others put in a word. The Colonel sat most of the time with his set, serious face, and his eye fixed as if he was not attending, though sometimes Kate found the quick keen brilliance of his look bent full upon her, so as to terrify her by its suddenness, and make her hardly know what she was saying or doing.

The worst moments were at dinner. She was, in the first place, sure that those dark questioning eyes had decided that there must be some sad cause for her not being trusted to drink her tea elsewhere; and then, in the pause after the first course, the eyes came again, and he said, and to her, "I hope your good relations the Wardours are well."

"Quite well--thank you," faltered Kate.

"When did you see them last?"

"A--a fortnight ago--" began Kate.

"Mr. Wardour came up to London for a few hours," said Lady Barbara, looking at Kate as if she meant to plunge her below the floor; at least, so the child imagined.

The sense that this was not the whole truth made her especially miserable; and all the rest of the evening was one misery of embarrassment, when her limbs did not seem to be her own, but as if somebody else was sitting at her little table, walking upstairs, and doing her work. Even Mrs. Umfraville's kind ways could not restore her; she only hung her head and mumbled when she was asked to show her work, and did not so much as know what was to become of her piece of cross-stitch when it was finished.

There was some inquiry after the De la Poers; and Mrs. Umfraville asked if she had found some playfellows among their daughters.

"Yes," faintly said Kate; and with another flush of colour, thought of having been told, that if Lady de la Poer knew what she had done, she would never be allowed to play with them again, and therefore that she never durst attempt it.

"They were very nice children," said Mrs. Umfraville.

"Remarkably nice children," returned Lady Barbara, in a tone that again cut Kate to the heart.

Bed-time came; and she would have been glad of it, but that all the time she was going to sleep there was the Lord Chancellor to think of, and the uncle and aunt with the statue faces dragging her before him.

Sunday was the next day, and the uncle and aunt were not seen till after the afternoon service, when they came to dinner, and much such an evening as the former one passed; but towards the end of it Mrs. Umfraville said, "Now, Barbara, I have a favour to ask. Will you let this child spend the day with me to-morrow? Giles will be out, and I shall be very glad to have her for my companion."

Kate's eyes glistened, and she thought of stern Proserpine.

"My dear Emily, you do not know what you ask. She will be far too much for you."

"I'll take care of that," said Mrs. Umfraville, smiling.

"And I don't know about trusting her. I cannot go out, and Jane cannot spare Bartley so early."

"I will come and fetch her," said the Colonel.

"And bring her back too. I will send the carriage in the evening, but do not let her come without you," said Lady Barbara earnestly.

Had they told, or would they tell after she was gone to bed? Kate thought Aunt Barbara was a woman of her word, but did not quite trust her. Consent was given; but would not that stern soldier destroy all the pleasure? And people in sorrow too! Kate thought of Mrs. Lacy, and had no very bright anticipations of her day; yet a holiday was something, and to be out of Aunt Barbara's way a great deal more.

She had not been long dressed when there was a ring at the bell, and, before she had begun to expect him, the tall man with the dark lip and grey hair stood in her schoolroom. She gave such a start, that he asked, "Did you not expect me so soon?"

"I did not think you would come till after breakfast: but--"

And with an impulse of running away from his dread presence, she darted off to put on her hat, but was arrested on the way by Lady Barbara, at her bedroom door.

"Uncle Giles is come for me," she said, and would have rushed on, but her aunt detained her to say, "Recollect, Katharine, that wildness and impetuosity, at all times unbecoming, are particularly so where there is affliction. If consideration for others will not influence you, bear in mind that on the impression you make on your uncle and aunt, it depends whether I shall be obliged to tell all that I would willingly forget."

Kate's heart swelled, and without speaking she entered her own room, thinking how hard it was to have even the pleasure of hoping for ease and enjoyment taken away.

When she came down, she found her aunt--as she believed--warning her uncle against her being left to herself; and then came, "If she should be too much for Emily, only send a note, and Bartley or I will come to fetch her home."

"She wants him to think me a little wild beast!" thought Kate; but her uncle answered, "Emily always knows how to deal with children. Good-bye."

"To deal with children! What did that mean?" thought the Countess, as she stepped along by the side of her uncle, not venturing to speak, and feeling almost as shy and bewildered as when she was on the world alone.

He did not speak, but when they came to a crossing of a main street, he took her by the hand; and there was something protecting and comfortable in the feel, so that she did not let go; and presently, as she walked on, she felt the fingers close on hers with such a quick tight squeeze, that she looked up in a fright and met the dark eye turned on her quite soft and glistening. She did not guess how he was thinking of little clasping hands that had held there before; and he only said something rather hurriedly about avoiding some coals that were being taken in through a round hole in the pavement.

Soon they were at the hotel; and Mrs. Umfraville came out of her room with that greeting which Kate liked so much, helped her to take off her cloak and smooth her hair, and then set her down to breakfast.

It was a silent meal to Kate. Her uncle and aunt had letters to read, and things to consult about that she did not understand; but all the time there was a kind watch kept up that she had what she liked; and Aunt Emily's voice was so much like the deep notes of the wood-pigeons round Oldburgh, that she did not care how long she listened to it, even if it had been talking Hindostanee!

As soon as breakfast was over, the Colonel took up his hat and went out; and

Mrs. Umfraville said, turning to Kate, "Now, my dear, I have something for you to help me in; I want to unpack some things that I have brought home."

"Oh, I shall like that!" said Kate, feeling as if a weight was gone with the grave uncle.

Mrs. Umfraville rang, and asked to have a certain box brought in. Such a box, all smelling of choice Indian wood; the very shavings that stuffed it were delightful! And what an unpacking! It was like nothing but the Indian stall at the Baker Street Bazaar! There were two beautiful large ivory work-boxes, inlaid with stripes and circles of tiny mosaic; and there were even more delicious little boxes of soft fragrant sandal wood, and a set of chessmen in ivory. The kings were riding on elephants, with canopies over their heads, and ladders to climb up by; and each elephant had a tiger in his trunk. Then the queens were not queens, but grand viziers, because the queen is nobody in the East: and each had a lesser elephant; the bishops were men riding on still smaller elephants; the castles had camels, the knights horses; and the pawns were little foot-soldiers, the white ones with guns, as being European troops, the red ones with bows and arrows. Kate was perfectly delighted with these men, and looked at and admired them one by one, longing to play a game with them. Then there was one of those wonderful clusters of Chinese ivory balls, all loose, one within the other, carved in different patterns of network, and there were shells spotted and pink-mouthed, card-cases, red shining boxes, queer Indian dolls; figures in all manner of costumes, in gorgeous colours, painted upon shining transparent talc or on soft rice-paper. There was no describing how charming the sight was, nor how Kate dwelt upon each article; and how pleasantly her aunt explained what it was intended for, and where it came from, answering all questions in the nicest, kindest way. When all the wool and shavings had been pinched, and the curled-up toes of the slippers explored, so as to make sure that no tiny shell nor ivory carving lurked unseen, the room looked like a museum; and Mrs. Umfraville said, "Most of these things were meant for our home friends: there is an Indian scarf and a Cashmere shawl for your two aunts, and I believe the chessmen are for Lord de la Poer."

"O Aunt Emily, I should so like to play one game with them before they go!"

"I will have one with you, if you can be very careful of their tender points," said Mrs. Umfraville, without one of the objections that Kate had expected; "but first I want you to help me about some of the other things. Your uncle meant one of the work-boxes for you!"

"O Aunt Emily, how delightful! I really will work, with such a dear beautiful box!" cried Kate, opening it, and again peeping into all its little holes and contrivances. "Here is the very place for a dormouse to sleep in! And who is the other for?"

"For Fanny de la Poer, who is his godchild."

"Oh, I am so glad! Fanny always has such nice pretty work about!"

"And now I want you to help me to choose the other presents. There; these," pointing to a scarf and a muslin dress adorned with the wings of diamond beetles, "are for some young cousins of my own; but you will be able best to choose what the other De la Poers and your cousins at Oldburgh would like best."

"My cousins at Oldburgh!" cried Kate. "May they have some of these pretty things?" And as her aunt answered "We hope they will," Kate flew at her, and hugged her quite tight round the throat; then, when Mrs. Umfraville undid the clasp, and returned the kiss, she went like an India-rubber ball with a backward bound, put her hands together over her head, and gasped out, "Oh, thank you, thank you!"

"My dear, don't go quite mad. You will jump into that calabash, and then it won't be fit for anybody. Are you so very glad?"

"Oh! so glad! Pretty things do come so seldom to Oldburgh!"

"Well, we thought you might like to send Miss Wardour this shawl."

It was a beautiful heavy shawl of the soft wool of the Cashmere goats; really of every kind of brilliant hue, but so dexterously blended together, that the whole looked dark and sober. But Kate did not look with favour on the shawl.

"A shawl is so stupid," she said. "If you please, I had rather Mary had the work-box."

"But the work-box is for Lady Fanny."

"Oh! but I meant my own," said Kate earnestly. "If you only knew what a pity it is to give nice things to me; they always get into such a mess. Now, Mary always has her things so nice; and she works so beautifully; she has never let Lily wear a stitch but of her setting; and she always wished for a box like this. One of her friends at school had a little one; and she used to say, when we played at roe's egg, that she wanted nothing but an ivory work-box; and she has nothing but an old blue one, with the steel turned black!"

"We must hear what your uncle says, for you must know that he meant the box for you."

"It isn't that I don't care for it," said Kate, with a sudden glistening in her eyes; "it is because I do care for it so very much that I want Mary to have it."

"I know it is, my dear;" and her aunt kissed her; "but we must think about it a little. Perhaps Mary would not think an Indian shawl quite so stupid as you do."

"Mary isn't a nasty vain conceited girl!" cried Kate indignantly. "She always looks nice; but I heard Papa say her dress did not cost much more than Sylvia's and mine, because she never tore anything, and took such care!"

"Well, we will see," said Mrs. Umfraville, perhaps not entirely convinced that the shawl would not be a greater prize to the thrifty girl than Kate perceived.

Kate meanwhile had sprung unmolested on a beautiful sandalwood case for Sylvia, and a set of rice-paper pictures for Lily; and the appropriating other treasures to the De la Poers, packing them up, and directing them, accompanied with explanations of their habits and tastes, lasted till so late, that after the litter was cleared away there was only time for one game at chess with the grand pieces; and in truth the honour of using them was greater than the pleasure. They covered up the board, so that there was no seeing the squares, and it was necessary to be most inconveniently cautious in lifting them. They were made to be looked at, not played with; and yet, wonderful to relate, Kate did not do one of the delicate things a mischief!

Was it that she was really grown more handy, or was it that with this gentle aunt she was quite at her ease, yet too much subdued to be careless and rough?

The luncheon came; and after it, she drove with her aunt first to a few shops, and then to take up the Colonel, who had been with his lawyer. Kate quaked a little inwardly, lest it should be about the Lord Chancellor, and tried to frame a question on the subject to her aunt; but even the most chattering little girls know what it is to have their lips sealed by an odd sort of reserve upon the very matters that make them most uneasy; and just because her wild imagination had been thinking that perhaps this was all a plot to waylay her into the Lord Chancellor's clutches, she could not utter a word on the matter, while they drove through the quiet squares where lawyers live.

Mrs. Umfraville, however, soon put that out of her head by talking to her about the Wardours, and setting open the flood gates of her eloquence about Sylvia. So delightful was it to have a listener, that Kate did not grow impatient, long as they waited at the lawyer's door in the dull square, and indeed was sorry when the Colonel made his appearance. He just said to her that he hoped she was not tired of waiting; and as she replied with a frightened little "No, thank you," began telling his wife something that Kate soon perceived belonged to his own concerns, not to hers; so she left off trying to gather the meaning in the rumble of the wheels, and looked out of window, for she could never be quite at ease when she felt that those eyes might be upon her.

On coming back to the hotel, Mrs. Umfraville found a note on the table for her: she read it, gave it to her husband, and said, "I had better go directly."

"Will it not be too much? Can you?" he said very low; and there was the same repressed twitching of the muscles of his face, as Kate had seen when he was left with his sister Jane.

"Oh yes!" she said fervently; "I shall like it. And it is her only chance; you see she goes to-morrow."

The carriage was ordered again, and Mrs. Umfraville explained to Kate that the note was from a poor invalid lady whose son was in their own regiment in India, that she was longing to hear about him, and was going out of town the next day.

"And what shall I give you to amuse yourself with, my dear?" asked Mrs. Umfraville. "I am afraid we have hardly a book that will suit you."

Kate had a great mind to ask to go and sit in the carriage, rather than remain alone with the terrible black moustache; but she was afraid of the Colonel's mentioning Aunt Barbara's orders that she was not to be let out of sight. "If you please," she said, "if I might write to Sylvia."

Her aunt kindly established her at a little table, with a leathern writing-case, and her uncle mended a pen for her. Then her aunt went away, and he sat down to his own letters.

Kate durst not speak to him, but she watched him under her eyelashes, and noticed how he presently laid down his pen, and gave a long, heavy, sad sigh, such as she had never heard when his wife was present; then sat musing, looking fixedly at the grey window; till, rousing himself with another such sigh, he seemed to force himself to go on writing, but paused again, as if he were so wearied and oppressed that he could hardly bear it.

It gave Kate a great awe of him, partly because a little girl in a book would have gone up, slid her hand into his, and kissed him; but she could nearly as soon have slid her hand into a lion's; and she was right, it would have been very obtrusive.

Some little time had passed before there was an opening of the door, and the announcement, "Lord de la Poer."

Up started Kate, but she was quite lost in the greeting of the two friends; Lord de la Poer, with his eyes full of tears, wringing his friend's hand, hardly able to speak, but just saying, "Dear Giles, I am glad to have you at home. How is she?"

"Wonderfully well," said the Colonel, with the calm voice but the twitching face. "She is gone to see Mrs. Ducie, the mother of a lad in my regiment, who was wounded at the same time as Giles, and whom she nursed with him."

"Is not it very trying?"

"Nothing that is a kindness ever is trying to Emily," he said, and his voice did tremble this time.

Kate had quietly re-seated herself in her chair. She felt that it was no moment to thrust herself in; nor did she feel herself aggrieved, even though unnoticed by such a favourite friend. Something in the whole spirit of the day had made her only sensible that she was a little girl, and quite forgot that she was a Countess.

The friends were much too intent on one another to think of her, as she sat in the recess of the window, their backs to her. They drew their chairs close to the fire, and began to talk, bending down together; and Kate felt sure, that as her uncle at least knew she was there, she need not interrupt. Besides, what they spoke of was what she had longed to hear, and would never have dared to ask. Lord de la Poer had been like a father to his friend's two sons when they were left in England; and now the Colonel was telling him--as, perhaps, he could have told no one else--about their brave spirit, and especially of Giles's patience and resolution through his lingering illness; how he had been entirely unselfish in entreating that anything might happen rather than that his father should resign his post; but though longing to be with his parents, and desponding as to his chance of recovery, had resigned himself in patience to whatever might be thought right; and how through the last sudden accession of illness brought on by the journey, his sole thought had been for his parents.

"And she has borne up!" said Lord de la Poer.

"As HE truly said, 'As long as she has anyone to care for, she will never break down.' Luckily, I was entirely knocked up for a few days just at first; and coming home we had a poor young woman on board very ill, and Emily nursed her day and night."

"And now you will bring her to Fanny and me to take care of."

"Thank you--another time. But, old fellow, I don't know whether we either of us could stand your house full of children yet. Emily would be always among them, and think she liked it; but I knew how it would be. It was just so when I took her to a kind friend of ours after the little girls were taken; she had the children constantly with her, but I never saw her so ill as she was afterwards."

"Reaction! Well, whenever you please; you shall have your rooms to your-selves, and only see us when you like. But I don't mean to press you; only, what are you going to do next?"

"I can hardly tell. There are business matters of our own, and about poor James's little girl, to keep us here a little while." ("Who is that?" thought Kate.)

"Then you must go into our house. I was in hopes it might be so, and told the housekeeper to make ready."

"Thank you; if Emily--We will see, when she comes in I want to make up my mind about that child. Have you seen much of her?"

Kate began to think honour required her to come forward, but her heart throbbed with fright.

"Not so much as I could wish. It is an intelligent little monkey, and our girls were delighted with her; but I believe Barbara thinks me a corrupter of youth, for she discountenances us."

"Ah! one of the last times I was alone with Giles, he said, smiling, 'That little girl in Bruton Street will be just what Mamma wants;' and I know Emily has never ceased to want to get hold of the motherless thing ever since Mrs. Wardour's death. I know it would be the greatest comfort to Emily, but I only doubted taking the child away from my sisters. I thought it would be such a happy thing to have Jane's kind heart drawn out; and if Barbara had forgiven the old sore, and used her real admirable good sense affectionately, it would have been like new life to them. Besides, it must make a great difference to their income. But is it possible that it can be the old prejudice, De la Poer? Barbara evidently dislikes the poor child, and treats her like a state prisoner!"

Honour prevailed entirely above fear and curiosity. Out flew Kate, to the exceeding amaze and discomfiture of the two gentlemen. "No, no, Uncle Giles; it is--it is because I ran away! Aunt Barbara said she would not tell, for if you knew it, you would--you would despise me;--and you," looking at Lord de la Poer, "would never let me play with Grace and Addy again!"

She covered her face with her hands--it was all burning red; and she was nearly rushing off, but she felt herself lifted tenderly upon a knee, and an arm round her. She thought it her old friend; but behold, it was her uncle's voice that said, in the softest gentlest way, "My dear, I never despise where I meet with truth. Tell me how it was; or had you rather tell your Aunt Emily?"

"I'll tell you," said Kate, all her fears softened by his touch. "Oh no! please don't go, Lord de la Poer; I do want you to know, for I couldn't have played with Grace and Adelaide on false pretences!" And encouraged by her uncle's tender pressure, she murmured out, "I ran away--I did--I went home!"

"To Oldburgh!"

"Yes--yes! It was very wrong; Papa--Uncle Wardour, I mean--made me see it was."

"And what made you do it?" said her uncle kindly. "Do not be afraid to tell me."

"It was because I was angry. Aunt Barbara would not let me go to the other Wardours, and wanted me to write a--what I thought--a fashionable falsehood; and when I said it was a lie," (if possible, Kate here became deeper crimson than she was before,) "she sent me to my room till I would beg her pardon, and write the note. So--so I got out of the house, and took a cab, and went home by the train. I didn't know it was so very dreadful a thing, or indeed I would not."

And Kate hid her burning face on her uncle's breast, and was considerably startled by what she heard next, from the Marquis.

"Hm! All I have to say is, that if Barbara had the keeping of me, I should run away at the end of a week."

"Probably!" and Lord de la Poer saw, what Kate did not, the first shadow of a smile on the face of his friend, as he pressed his arm round the still trembling girl; "but, you see, Barbara justly thinks you corrupt youth.--My little girl, you must not let HIM make you think lightly of this--"

"Oh, no, I never could! Papa was so shocked!" and she was again covered with confusion at the thought.

"But," added her uncle, "it is not as if you had not gone to older and better friends than any you have ever had, my poor child. I am afraid you have been much tried, and have not had a happy life since you left Oldburgh."

"I have always been naughty," said Kate.

"Then we must try if your Aunt Emily can help you to be good. Will you try to be as like her own child to her as you can, Katharine?"

"And to you," actually whispered Kate; for somehow at that moment she cared much more for the stern uncle than the gentle aunt.

He lifted her up and kissed her, but set her down again with the sigh that told how little she could make up to him for the son he had left in Egypt. Yet, perhaps that sigh made Kate long with more fervent love for some way of being so very good and affectionate as quite to make him happy, than if he had received her demonstration as if satisfied by it.

CHAPTER XV.

Nothing of note passed during the rest of the evening. Mrs. Umfraville came home; but Kate had fallen back into the shy fit that rendered her unwilling to begin on what was personal, and the Colonel waited to talk it over with his wife alone before saying any more.

Besides, there were things far more near to them than their little great-niece, and Mrs. Umfraville could not see Lord de la Poer without having her heart very full of the sons to whom he had been so kind. Again they sat round the fire, and this time in the dark, while once more Giles and Frank and all their ways were talked over and over, and Kate was forgotten; but she was not sitting alone in the dark window--no, she had a footstool close to her uncle, and sat resting her head upon his knee, her eyes seeking red caverns in the coals, her heart in a strange peaceful rest, her ears listening to the mother's subdued tender tones in speaking of her boys, and the friend's voice of sympathy and affection. Her uncle leant back and did not speak at all; but the other two went on and on, and Mrs. Umfraville seemed to be drinking in every little trait of her boys' English life, not weeping over it, but absolutely smiling when it was something droll or characteristic.

Kate felt subdued and reverent, and loved her new relations more and more for their sorrows; and she began to dream out castles of the wonderful goodness by which she would comfort them; then she looked for her uncle's hand to see if she could dare to stroke it, but one was over his brow, the other out of reach, and she was shy of doing anything.

The dinner interrupted them; and Kate had the pleasure of dining late, and sitting opposite to Lord de la Poer, who talked now and then to her, and told her what Adelaide and Grace were doing; but he was grave and sad, out of sympathy with his friends, and Kate was by no means tempted to be foolish.

Indeed, she began to feel that she might hope to be always good with her uncle and aunt, and that they would never make her naughty. Only too soon came the announcement of the carriage for Lady Caergwent; and when Aunt Emily took her into the bedroom to dress, she clung to that kind hand and fondled it.

"My dear little girl!" and Aunt Emily held her in her arms, "I am so glad! Kate, I do think your dear uncle is a little cheered to-night! If having you about him does him any good, how I shall love you, Katie!" and she hugged her closer. "And it is so kind in Lord de la Poer to have come! Oh, now he will be better! I am so thankful he is in England again! You must be with us whenever Barbara can spare you, Katie dear, for I am sure he likes it."

"Each wants me, to do the other good," thought Kate; and she was so much touched and pleased that she did not know what to do, and looked foolish.

Uncle Giles took her down stairs; and when they were in the carriage, in the dark, he seemed to be less shy: he lifted her on his knee and said, "I will talk to your aunt, and we will see how soon you can come to us, my dear."

"Oh, do let it be soon," said Kate.

"That must depend upon your Aunt Barbara," he answered, "and upon law matters, perhaps. And you must not be troublesome to her; she has suffered very much, and will not think of herself, so you must think for her."

"I don't know how, Uncle Giles," said poor sincere Kate. "At home, they always said I had no consideration."

"You must learn," he said gravely. "She is not to be harassed."

Kate was rather frightened; but he spoke in a kinder voice. "At home, you say. Do you mean with my sisters, or at Oldburgh?"

"Oh, at Oldburgh, Uncle Giles!"

"You are older now," he answered, "and need not be so childish."

"And please one thing--"

"Well--"

There came a great choking in her throat, but she did get it out. "Please, please, don't think all I do wrong is the Wardours' fault! I know I am naughty and horrid and unladylike, but it is my own own fault, indeed it is, and nobody ELSE'S! Mary and Uncle Wardour would have made me good--and it was all my fault."

"My dear," and he put the other hand so that he completely encircled the little slim waist, "I do quite believe that Mr. Wardour taught you all the good you have. There is nothing I am so glad of as that you love and reverence him as he deserves- -as far as such a child can do. I hope you always will, and that your gratitude will increase with your knowledge of the sacrifices that he made for you."

It was too much of a speech for Kate to answer; but she nestled up to him, and felt as if she loved him more than ever. He added, "I should like to see Mr. Wardour, but I can hardly leave your aunt yet. Would he come to London?"

Kate gave a gasp. "Oh dear! Sylvia said he would have no money for journeys now! It cost so much his coming in a first-class carriage with me."

"You see how necessary it is to learn consideration," said the Colonel; "I must run down to see him, and come back at night."

By this time they were at the aunts' door, and both entered the drawing-room together.

Lady Barbara anxiously hoped that Katharine had behaved well.

"Perfectly well," he answered; and his face was really brighter and tenderer.

It was Kate's bed-time, and she was dismissed at once. She felt that the kiss and momentary touch of the hand, with the "Bless you," were far more earnest than the mere greeting kiss. She did not know that it had been his wonted good-night to his own children.

When she was gone, he took a chair, and explained that he could remain for a little while, as Lord de la Poer would bear his wife company. Lady Jane made room for him on the sofa, and Lady Barbara looked pleased.

"I wished to talk to you about that child," he said.

"I have been wishing it for some time," said Lady Barbara; "waiting, in fact, to make arrangements till your return."

"What arrangements?"

"For forming an establishment for her."

"The child's natural home is with you or with me."

There was a little silence; then Lady Jane nervously caught her brother's hand, saying, "O Giles, Giles, you must not be severe with her, poor little thing!"

"Why should I be severe, Jane?" he said. "What has the child done to deserve it?"

"I do not wish to enter into particulars," said Lady Barbara. "But she is a child who has been so unfortunately brought up as to require constant watching; and to have her in the house does so much harm to Jane's health, that I strongly advise you not to attempt it in Emily's state of spirits."

"It would little benefit Emily's spirits to transfer a duty to a stranger," said the Colonel. "But I wish to know why you evidently think so ill of this girl, Barbara!"

"Her entire behaviour since she has been with us--" began Lady Barbara.

"Generalities only do mischief, Barbara. If I have any control over this child, I must know facts."

"The truth is, Giles," said his sister, distressed and confused, "that I promised the child not to tell you of her chief piece of misconduct, unless I was compelled by some fresh fault."

"An injudicious promise, Barbara. You do the child more harm by implying such an opinion of her than you could do by letting me hear what she has actually done. But you are absolved from the promise, for she has herself told me."

"Told you! That girl has no sense of shame! After all the pains I took to conceal it!"

"No, Barbara; it was with the utmost shame that she told me. It was unguarded of me, I own; but De la Poer and I had entirely forgotten that she was present, and I asked him if he could account for your evident dislike and distrust of her. The child's honourable feelings would not allow her to listen, and she came forward, and accused herself, not you!"

"Before Lord de la Poer! Giles, how could you allow it?" cried Lady Barbara, confounded. "That whole family will tell the story, and she will be marked for ever!"

"De la Poer has some knowledge of child nature," said the Colonel, slightly smiling.

"A gentleman often encourages that sort of child, but condemns her the more. She will be a by-word in that family! I always knew she would be our disgrace!"

"O Giles, do tell Barbara it cannot be so very bad!" entreated Lady Jane. "She is such a child--poor little dear!--and so little used to control!"

"I have only as yet heard her own confused account."

Lady Barbara gave her own.

"I see," said the Colonel, "the child was both accurate and candid. You should be thankful that your system has not destroyed her sincerity."

"But, indeed, dear Giles," pleaded Lady Jane, "you know Barbara did not want her to say what was false."

"No," said the Colonel: "that was a mere misunderstanding. It is the spirit of distrust that--assuming that a child will act dishonourably--is likely to drive her to do so."

"I never distrusted Katharine till she drove me to do so," said Lady Barbara, with cold, stern composure.

"I would never bring an accusation of breach of trust where I had not made it evident that I reposed confidence," said the Colonel.

"I see how it is," said Lady Barbara; "you have heard one side. I do not contradict. I know the girl would not wilfully deceive by word; and I am willing to confess that I am not capable of dealing with her. Only from a sense of duty did I ever undertake it."

"Of duty, Barbara?" he asked.

"Yes--of duty to the family."

"We do not see those things in the same light," he said quietly. "I thought, as you know, that the duty was more incumbent when the child was left an orphan--a burthen on relatives who could ill afford to be charged with her. Perhaps, Barbara, if you had noticed her THEN, instead of waiting till circumstances made her the head of our family, you might have been able to give her that which has been wanting in your otherwise conscientious training--affection."

Lady Barbara held up her head, stiffly, but she was very near tears, of pain and wounded pride; but she would not defend herself; and she saw that even her faithful Jane did not feel with her.

"I came home, Barbara," continued the Colonel, "resolving that--much as I wished for Emily's sake that this little girl should need a home with us--if you had found in her a new interest and delight, and were in her--let me say it, Barbara--healing old sores, and giving her your own good sense and high principle, I would not say one word to disturb so happy a state of things. I come and find the child a state prisoner, whom you are endeavouring by all means to alienate from the friends to whom she owes a daughter's gratitude; I find her not complaining of you, but answering me with the saddest account a child can give of herself--she is always naughty. After this, Barbara, I can be doing you no injury in asking you to concur with me in arrangements for putting the child under my wife's care as soon as possible."

"To-morrow, if you like," said Lady Barbara. "I took her only from a sense of duty; and it has half killed Jane. I would not keep her upon any consideration!"

"O Barbara, it has not hurt me.--O Giles, she will always be so anxious about me; it is all my fault for being nervous and foolish!" cried Lady Jane, with quivering voice, and tears in her eyes. "If it had not been for that, we could have made her so happy, dear little spirited thing. But dear Barbara spoils me, and I know I give way too much."

"This will keep you awake all night!" said Barbara, as the Colonel's tender gesture agitated Jane more. "Indeed, Giles, you should have chosen a better moment for this conversation--on almost your first arrival too! But the very existence of this child is a misfortune!"

"Let us trust that in a few years she may give you reason to think otherwise," said the Colonel. "Did you mean what you said--that you wished us to take her to-morrow?"

"Not to incommode Emily. She can go on as she has done till your plans are made. You do not know what a child she is."

"Emily shall come and settle with you to-morrow," said Colonel Umfraville. "I have not yet spoken to her, but I think she will wish to have the child with her."

"And you will be patient with her. You will make her happy," said Lady Jane, holding his hand.

"Everything is made happy by Emily," he answered.

"But has she spirits for the charge?"

"She has always spirits enough to give happiness to others," he answered; and the dew was on his dark lashes.

"And you, Giles--you will not be severe even if the poor child is a little wild?"

"I know what you are thinking of, Jane," he said kindly. "But indeed, my dear, such a wife as mine, and such sorrows as she has helped me to bear, would have been wasted indeed, if by God's grace they had not made me less exacting and impatient than I used to be.-- Barbara," he added after a pause, "I beg your pardon if I have spoken hastily, or done you injustice. All you have done has been conscientious; and if I spoke in displeasure--you know how one's spirit is moved by seeing a child unhappy--and my training in gentleness is not as complete as it ought to be, I am sorry for the pain I gave you."

Lady Barbara was struggling with tears she could not repress; and at last she broke quite down, and wept so that Lady Jane moved about in alarm and distress, and her brother waited in some anxiety. But when she spoke it was humbly.

"You were right, Giles. It was not in me to love that child. It was wrong in me. Perhaps if I had overcome the feeling when you first told me of it, when her mother died, it would have been better for us all. Now it is too late. Our habits have formed themselves, and I can neither manage the child nor make her happy. It is better that she should go to you and Emily. And, Giles, if you still bring her to us sometimes, I will try--" The last words were lost.

"You will," he said affectionately, "when there are no more daily collisions. Dear Barbara, if I am particularly anxious to train this poor girl up at once in affection and in self-restraint, it is because my whole life--ever since I grew up--has taught me what a grievous task is left us, after we are our own masters. If our childish faults--such as impetuosity and sullenness--are not corrected on principle, not for convenience, while we are children."

After this conversation, everyone will be sure that Mrs. Umfraville came next day, and after many arrangements with Lady Barbara, carried off the little Countess with her to the house that Lord de la Poer had lent them.

Kate was subdued and quiet. She felt that she had made a very unhappy business of her life with her aunts, and that she should never see Bruton Street without a sense of shame. Lady Barbara, too, was more soft and kind than she had ever seen her; and Aunt Jane was very fond of her, and grieved over her not having been happier.

"Oh, never mind, Aunt Jane; it was all my naughtiness. I know Aunt Emily will make me good; and nobody could behave ill in the house with Uncle Giles, could they now? So I shall be sure to be happy. And I'll tell you what, Aunt Jane; some day you shall come to stay with us, and then I'll drive you out in a dear delicious open carriage, with two prancing ponies!"

And when she wished her other aunt good-bye, she eased her mind by saying, "Aunt Barbara, I am very sorry I was such a horrid plague."

"There were faults on both sides, Katharine," her aunt answered with dignity. "Perhaps in time we may understand one another better."

The first thing Katharine heard when she had left the house with Mrs. Umfraville was, that her uncle had gone down to Oldburgh by an early train, and that both box and shawl had gone with him.

But when he came back late to Lord de la Poer's house, whom had he brought with him?

Mary! Mary Wardour herself! He had, as a great favour, begged to have her for a fortnight in London, to take care of her little cousin, till further arrangements could be made; and to talk over with Mrs. Umfraville the child's character, and what would be good for her.

If there was one shy person in the house that night, there was another happier than words could tell!

Moreover, before very long, the Countess of Caergwent had really seen the Lord Chancellor, and found him not so very unlike other people after all; indeed, unless Uncle Giles had told her, she never would have found out who he was! And when he asked her whether she would wish to live with Colonel Umfraville or with Lady Barbara and Lady Jane, it may be very easily guessed what answer she made!

So it was fixed that she should live at Caergwent Castle with her uncle and aunt, and be brought up to the care of her own village and poor people, and to learn the duties of her station under their care.

And before they left London, Mrs. Umfraville had chosen a very bright pleasant young governess, to be a friend and companion, as well as an instructress. Further, it was settled that as soon as Christmas was over, Sylvia should come for a long visit, and learn of the governess with Kate.

Those who have learned to know Countess Kate can perhaps guess whether she found herself right in thinking it impossible to be naughty near Uncle Giles or Aunt Emily. But of one thing they may be sure--that Uncle Giles never failed to make her truly sorry for her naughtiness, and increasingly earnest in the struggle to leave it off.

And as time went on, and occupations and interests grew up round Colonel and Mrs. Umfraville, and their niece lost her childish wildness, and loved them more and more, they felt their grievous loss less and less, and did not so miss the vanished earthly hope. Their own children had so lived that they could feel them safe; and they attached themselves to the child in their charge till she was really like their own.

Yet, all the time, Kate still calls Mr. Wardour "Papa;" and Sylvia spends half her time with her. Some people still say that in manners, looks, and ways, Sylvia would make a better Countess than Lady Caergwent; but there are things that both are learning together, which alone can make them fit for any lot upon earth, or for the better inheritance in Heaven.

The Codes Of Hammurabi And Moses
W. W. Davies

QTY

The discovery of the Hammurabi Code is one of the greatest achievements of archaeology, and is of paramount interest, not only to the student of the Bible, but also to all those interested in ancient history...

Religion   ISBN: *1-59462-338-4*   Pages:132

MSRP *$12.95*

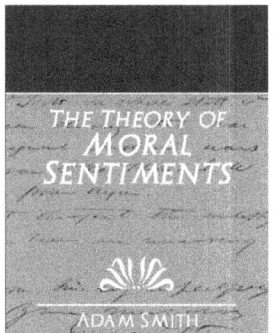

The Theory of Moral Sentiments
Adam Smith

QTY

This work from 1749. contains original theories of conscience amd moral judgment and it is the foundation for systemof morals.

Philosophy ISBN: *1-59462-777-0*   Pages:536

MSRP *$19.95*

Jessica's First Prayer
Hesba Stretton

QTY

In a screened and secluded corner of one of the many railway-bridges which span the streets of London there could be seen a few years ago, from five o'clock every morning until half past eight, a tidily set-out coffee-stall, consisting of a trestle and board, upon which stood two large tin cans, with a small fire of charcoal burning under each so as to keep the coffee boiling during the early hours of the morning when the work-people were thronging into the city on their way to their daily toil...

Childrens   ISBN: *1-59462-373-2*   Pages:84

MSRP *$9.95*

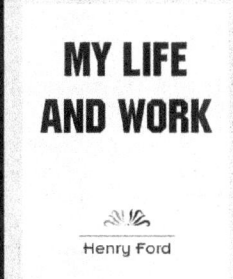

My Life and Work
Henry Ford

QTY

Henry Ford revolutionized the world with his implementation of mass production for the Model T automobile. Gain valuable business insight into his life and work with his own auto-biography... "We have only started on our development of our country we have not as yet, with all our talk of wonderful progress, done more than scratch the surface. The progress has been wonderful enough but..."

Biographies/ ISBN: *1-59462-198-5*   Pages:300

MSRP *$21.95*

The Art of Cross-Examination
Francis Wellman

QTY

I presume it is the experience of every author, after his first book is published upon an important subject, to be almost overwhelmed with a wealth of ideas and illustrations which could readily have been included in his book, and which to his own mind, at least, seem to make a second edition inevitable. Such certainly was the case with me; and when the first edition had reached its sixth impression in five months, I rejoiced to learn that it seemed to my publishers that the book had met with a sufficiently favorable reception to justify a second and considerably enlarged edition. ...

Reference   **ISBN:** *1-59462-647-2*

Pages:412

MSRP $19.95

On the Duty of Civil Disobedience
Henry David Thoreau

QTY

Thoreau wrote his famous essay, On the Duty of Civil Disobedience, as a protest against an unjust but popular war and the immoral but popular institution of slave-owning. He did more than write—he declined to pay his taxes, and was hauled off to gaol in consequence. Who can say how much this refusal of his hastened the end of the war and of slavery ?

Law   **ISBN:** *1-59462-747-9*

Pages:48

MSRP $7.45

Dream Psychology Psychoanalysis for Beginners
Sigmund Freud

QTY

Sigmund Freud, born Sigismund Schlomo Freud (May 6, 1856 - September 23, 1939), was a Jewish-Austrian neurologist and psychiatrist who co-founded the psychoanalytic school of psychology. Freud is best known for his theories of the unconscious mind, especially involving the mechanism of repression; his redefinition of sexual desire as mobile and directed towards a wide variety of objects; and his therapeutic techniques, especially his understanding of transference in the therapeutic relationship and the presumed value of dreams as sources of insight into unconscious desires.

Psychology   **ISBN:** *1-59462-905-6*

Pages:196

MSRP $15.45

The Miracle of Right Thought
Orison Swett Marden

QTY

Believe with all of your heart that you will do what you were made to do. When the mind has once formed the habit of holding cheerful, happy, prosperous pictures, it will not be easy to form the opposite habit. It does not matter how improbable or how far away this realization may see, or how dark the prospects may be, if we visualize them as best we can, as vividly as possible, hold tenaciously to them and vigorously struggle to attain them, they will gradually become actualized, realized in the life. But a desire, a longing without endeavor, a yearning abandoned or held indifferently will vanish without realization.

Pages:360

Self Help   **ISBN:** *1-59462-644-8*

MSRP $25.45

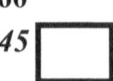

The Rosicrucian Cosmo-Conception Mystic Christianity *by Max Heindel*   ISBN: *1-59462-188-8*   **$38.95**
The Rosicrucian Cosmo-conception is not dogmatic, neither does it appeal to any other authority than the reason of the student. It is: not controversial, but is: sent forth in the, hope that it may help to clear...   New Age/Religion Pages 646

Abandonment To Divine Providence *by Jean-Pierre de Caussade*   ISBN: *1-59462-228-0*   **$25.95**
"The Rev. Jean Pierre de Caussade was one of the most remarkable spiritual writers of the Society of Jesus in France in the 18th Century. His death took place at Toulouse in 1751. His works have gone through many editions and have been republished...   Inspirational/Religion Pages 400

Mental Chemistry *by Charles Haanel*   ISBN: *1-59462-192-6*   **$23.95**
Mental Chemistry allows the change of material conditions by combining and appropriately utilizing the power of the mind. Much like applied chemistry creates something new and unique out of careful combinations of chemicals the mastery of mental chemistry...   New Age Pages 354

The Letters of Robert Browning and Elizabeth Barret Barrett 1845-1846 vol II   ISBN: *1-59462-193-4*   **$35.95**
by Robert Browning and Elizabeth Barrett   Biographies Pages 596

Gleanings In Genesis (volume I) *by Arthur W. Pink*   ISBN: *1-59462-130-6*   **$27.45**
Appropriately has Genesis been termed "the seed plot of the Bible" for in it we have, in germ form, almost all of the great doctrines which are afterwards fully developed in the books of Scripture which follow...   Religion/Inspirational Pages 420

The Master Key *by L. W. de Laurence*   ISBN: *1-59462-001-6*   **$30.95**
In no branch of human knowledge has there been a more lively increase of the spirit of research during the past few years than in the study of Psychology, Concentration and Mental Discipline. The requests for authentic lessons in Thought Control, Mental Discipline and...   New Age/Business Pages 422

The Lesser Key Of Solomon Goetia *by L. W. de Laurence*   ISBN: *1-59462-092-X*   **$9.95**
This translation of the first book of the "Lernegton" which is now for the first time made accessible to students of Talismanic Magic was done, after careful collation and edition, from numerous Ancient Manuscripts in Hebrew, Latin, and French...   New Age/Occult Pages 92

Rubaiyat Of Omar Khayyam *by Edward Fitzgerald*   ISBN:*1-59462-332-5*   **$13.95**
Edward Fitzgerald, whom the world has already learned, in spite of his own efforts to remain within the shadow of anonymity, to look upon as one of the rarest poets of the century, was born at Bredfield, in Suffolk, on the 31st of March, 1809. He was the third son of John Purcell...   Music Pages 172

Ancient Law *by Henry Maine*   ISBN: *1-59462-128-4*   **$29.95**
The chief object of the following pages is to indicate some of the earliest ideas of mankind, as they are reflected in Ancient Law, and to point out the relation of those ideas to modern thought.   Religiom/History Pages 452

Far-Away Stories *by William J. Locke*   ISBN: *1-59462-129-2*   **$19.45**
"Good wine needs no bush, but a collection of mixed vintages does. And this book is just such a collection. Some of the stories I do not want to remain buried for ever in the museum files of dead magazine-numbers an author's not unpardonable vanity..."   Fiction Pages 272

Life of David Crockett *by David Crockett*   ISBN: *1-59462-250-7*   **$27.45**
"Colonel David Crockett was one of the most remarkable men of the times in which he lived. Born in humble life, but gifted with a strong will, an indomitable courage, and unremitting perseverance...   Biographies/New Age Pages 424

Lip-Reading *by Edward Nitchie*   ISBN: *1-59462-206-X*   **$25.95**
Edward B. Nitchie, founder of the New York School for the Hard of Hearing, now the Nitchie School of Lip-Reading, Inc, wrote "LIP-READING Principles and Practice". The development and perfecting of this meritorious work on lip-reading was an undertaking...   How-to Pages 400

A Handbook of Suggestive Therapeutics, Applied Hypnotism, Psychic Science   ISBN: *1-59462-214-0*   **$24.95**
by Henry Munro   Health/New Age/Health/Self-help Pages 376

A Doll's House: and Two Other Plays *by Henrik Ibsen*   ISBN: *1-59462-112-8*   **$19.95**
Henrik Ibsen created this classic when in revolutionary 1848 Rome. Introducing some striking concepts in playwriting for the realist genre, this play has been studied the world over.   Fiction/Classics/Plays 308

The Light of Asia *by sir Edwin Arnold*   ISBN: *1-59462-204-3*   **$13.95**
In this poetic masterpiece, Edwin Arnold describes the life and teachings of Buddha. The man who was to become known as Buddha to the world was born as Prince Gautama of India but he rejected the worldly riches and abandoned the reigns of power when...   Religion/History/Biographies Pages 170

The Complete Works of Guy de Maupassant *by Guy de Maupassant*   ISBN: *1-59462-157-8*   **$16.95**
"For days and days, nights and nights, I had dreamed of that first kiss which was to consecrate our engagement, and I knew not on what spot I should put my lips..."   Fiction/Classics Pages 240

The Art of Cross-Examination *by Francis L. Wellman*   ISBN: *1-59462-309-0*   **$26.95**
Written by a renowned trial lawyer, Wellman imparts his experience and uses case studies to explain how to use psychology to extract desired information through questioning.   How-to/Science/Reference Pages 408

Answered or Unanswered? *by Louisa Vaughan*   ISBN: *1-59462-248-5*   **$10.95**
Miracles of Faith in China   Religion Pages 112

The Edinburgh Lectures on Mental Science (1909) *by Thomas*   ISBN: *1-59462-008-3*   **$11.95**
This book contains the substance of a course of lectures recently given by the writer in the Queen Street Hall, Edinburgh. Its purpose is to indicate the Natural Principles governing the relation between Mental Action and Material Conditions...   New Age/Psychology Pages 148

Ayesha *by H. Rider Haggard*   ISBN: *1-59462-301-5*   **$24.95**
Verily and indeed it is the unexpected that happens! Probably if there was one person upon the earth from whom the Editor of this, and of a certain previous history, did not expect to hear again...   Classics Pages 380

Ayala's Angel *by Anthony Trollope*   ISBN: *1-59462-352-X*   **$29.95**
The two girls were both pretty, but Lucy who was twenty-one who supposed to be simple and comparatively unattractive, whereas Ayala was credited, as her Bombwhat romantic name might show, with poetic charm and a taste for romance. Ayala when her father died was nineteen...   Fiction Pages 484

The American Commonwealth *by James Bryce*   ISBN: *1-59462-286-8*   **$34.45**
An interpretation of American democratic political theory. It examines political mechanics and society from the perspective of Scotsman James Bryce   Politics Pages 572

Stories of the Pilgrims *by Margaret P. Pumphrey*   ISBN: *1-59462-116-0*   **$17.95**
This book explores pilgrims religious oppression in England as well as their escape to Holland and eventual crossing to America on the Mayflower, and their early days in New England...   History Pages 268

QTY

The Fasting Cure *by Sinclair Upton*   ISBN: *1-59462-222-1*   **$13.95**

*In the Cosmopolitan Magazine for May, 1910, and in the Contemporary Review (London) for April, 1910, I published an article dealing with my experi-
ences in fasting. I have written a great many magazine articles, but never one which attracted so much attention... New Age/Self Help/Health Pages 164*

Hebrew Astrology *by Sepharial*   ISBN: *1-59462-308-2*   **$13.45**

*In these days of advanced thinking it is a matter of common observation that we have left many of the old landmarks behind and that we are now pressing
forward to greater heights and to a wider horizon than that which represented the mind-content of our progenitors...   Astrology Pages 144*

Thought Vibration or The Law of Attraction in the Thought World   ISBN: *1-59462-127-6*   **$12.95**

by William Walker Atkinson   *Psychology/Religion Pages 144*

Optimism *by Helen Keller*   ISBN: *1-59462-108-X*   **$15.95**

*Helen Keller was blind, deaf, and mute since 19 months old, yet famously learned how to overcome these handicaps, communicate with the world, and
spread her lectures promoting optimism. An inspiring read for everyone...   Biographies/Inspirational Pages 84*

Sara Crewe *by Frances Burnett*   ISBN: *1-59462-360-0*   **$9.45**

*In the first place, Miss Minchin lived in London. Her home was a large, dull, tall one, in a large, dull square, where all the houses were alike, and all the
sparrows were alike, and where all the door-knockers made the same heavy sound...   Childrens/Classic Pages 88*

The Autobiography of Benjamin Franklin *by Benjamin Franklin*   ISBN: *1-59462-135-7*   **$24.95**

*The Autobiography of Benjamin Franklin has probably been more extensively read than any other American historical work, and no other book of its kind
has had such ups and downs of fortune. Franklin lived for many years in England, where he was agent...   Biographies/History Pages 332*

Name	
Email	
Telephone	
Address	
City, State ZIP	

☐ **Credit Card**   ☐ **Check / Money Order**

Credit Card Number	
Expiration Date	
Signature	

Please Mail to: Book Jungle
PO Box 2226
Champaign, IL 61825
or Fax to: *630-214-0564*

ORDERING INFORMATION

web*: www.bookjungle.com*
email*: sales@bookjungle.com*
fax*: 630-214-0564*
mail*: Book Jungle PO Box 2226 Champaign, IL 61825*
or PayPal *to sales@bookjungle.com*

Please contact us for bulk discounts

DIRECT-ORDER TERMS

**20% Discount if You Order
Two or More Books**
Free Domestic Shipping!
Accepted: Master Card, Visa,
Discover, American Express